HUNTER'S MOON

A HARRY STARKE & KATE GAZZARA NOVEL

BLAIR HOWARD

For Jo, my ever-loving wife of 44 years

1

————

Night Watch

Sunday Morning 2am

It was one of those nights when I couldn't sleep. October Friday nights in Chattanooga can be restless, especially during a rare Hunter's Moon, and I found myself walking along the riverfront at two in the morning. The Tennessee River moved slowly, like black silk beneath the orange glow of the full moon, and the air carried that peculiar chill that comes just before autumn surrenders to winter.

That's when I noticed the gathering police cars at the Tennessee Aquarium, their red and blue lights reflecting off the water like some kind of twisted light show. Even from three blocks away, I could tell this wasn't a routine call. Too many units, too much activity for a simple break-in or vandalism. Something significant had happened at one of Chattanooga's most prominent landmarks.

I pulled out my phone and called Kate Gazzara. We friends for over twenty years, since she was fresh out University of Tennessee with a degree in forensic psycho and more determination than anyone had a right to possess something unusual was happening at the aquarium, I figure she'd know what was going on.

"Harry?" Kate's voice sounded tired but alert. "Please tell me you're not calling because you can't sleep and want to chat about Amanda's latest story assignment."

"I'm standing on the riverfront looking at what appears to be half the Chattanooga Police Department surrounding the aquarium," I said. "I thought you might want to know your Saturday night just got more complicated."

There was a pause, then the sound of Kate getting out of bed. "I'll be there in thirty minutes. Don't go inside until I arrive, and don't let anyone see you. If this turns into something that needs your particular expertise, well, we'll see."

"Understood. I'll stay in the shadows until you get here."

Thirty-five minutes later, Kate and I and Samson, her ever-present K-9 partner, were standing outside the aquarium's main entrance, watching the controlled chaos that accompanies any major crime scene. Kate looked every inch the professional despite being roused from sleep—her long, blonde hair pulled back in a ponytail, wearing jeans and a tan leather jacket over a white t-shirt. At thirty-nine, she carried herself with all the confidence of someone who'd earned her captain's bars through competence rather than politics.

"What do we know?" I asked.

"One of the security guards found a body floating in one of the exhibits sometime around midnight," Kate replied, checking her phone for updates. "The first responding officers called for backup and sealed the building."

Kate badged her way past the perimeter officers, bringing me with her. It was an arrangement we'd developed over the years. Back in the day, when I was a cop, she'd been assigned to me as my partner. She was still a rookie then, and for the next six years until I resigned from the force in 2008, I'd trained her. Thus it was that from time to time, she'd call me in as a consultant, but only with the chief's authorization, and always without pay. During the years since, we'd solved more than a dozen cases together, cases that might have remained mysteries had we not joined forces, so to speak.

I'd been to the aquarium many times, but at night the interior had a whole different feel to it. During operating hours, it bustled with families and school groups, filled with the sounds of children's laughter and the gentle hum of massive filtration systems. Now it seemed almost cathedral-like in its silence, the only illumination coming from the blue-green glow of the exhibit tanks and harsh police floodlights.

Security guard Frank Williams, a nervous man in his fifties with thinning gray hair and a slight tremor in his hands, met us at the main information desk. It was he who had made the discovery, and the shock hadn't worn off yet.

"I've worked security here for eight years," Williams said, his voice shaky. "Never seen anything like this. Never wanted to see anything like this."

Kate took out her notebook. "Walk us through it, Mr. Williams. Take your time."

"Well, I was back here, see?" Williams said as he led us deeper into the facility, past the river otters and through the butterfly garden, toward the Ocean Journey exhibit. The deeper we went, the more uneasy I became. There was something in the air, not just the usual aquarium smells of salt water and marine life, but something else. Something felt...

wrong. I looked at Samson. His ears were slightly flattened, the fur on the back of his neck was raised, and he was looking around as he trotted along beside Kate.

"I was making my regular rounds," Williams continued. "Everything was normal until I got to the sea turtle habitat. That's when I saw..." He stopped walking and pointed ahead to the massive glass window of the Neptune exhibit. "That's when I saw her. It's Jennifer! Dr. Parker."

"Dr. Parker?" Kate asked. "Is she a member of the staff?"

"Sort of," he replied. "She helps maintain the correct environment in the tanks. Well, she did. She's also a professor at UTC. Some sort of biologist, I think."

We were to find out later that she was actually Professor of environmental toxicology.

The Neptune exhibit—a massive tank containing thousands of gallons of carefully maintained salt water—was home to a rescued green sea turtle named Neptune.

Suspended in the clear water like some grotesque parody of synchronized swimming, was the body of a woman. She was floating face-down—Neptune slowly circling her—her long dark hair spreading around her head like seaweed, her arms extended as if she were reaching for something just beyond her grasp.

"Geez," I whispered.

Samson stopped dead and stared up at the body, his hackles raised, and he began pacing back and forth in front of the exhibit with the kind of restless energy that suggested he sensed something beyond the obvious tragedy. Samson had been Kate's partner for three years, and his instincts were usually reliable.

"Easy, boy," Kate murmured, but she was watching Samson

carefully. The dog's behavior meant there were elements in this scene that weren't immediately apparent.

I walked the front of the tank, looking for details that might explain how the woman had ended up dead in the exhibit.

The Neptune exhibit, a reef habitat, was one of the aquarium's crown jewels—a massive forty-foot long by twelve feet high expanse of carefully constructed coral formations that housed a thriving ecosystem of marine life. Artificial and living corals created a maze of caves, overhangs, and crevices where dozens of tropical fish darted in brilliant flashes of yellow, blue, and orange. A large moray eel had made its home in the shadowy nether recesses of the reef, while two Caribbean reef octopuses claimed territories among the rocky outcroppings.

But the undisputed star of the exhibit was Neptune, a massive green sea turtle whose ancient, weathered shell and wise eyes had captivated visitors for over a decade. At nearly five feet long and weighing close to three hundred pounds, Neptune commanded the space with the dignity of a king surveying his domain. He was beloved by staff and visitors alike, and known for his gentle nature and curious habit of swimming up to the glass whenever children approached.

The reef was designed to showcase the interconnected nature of marine ecosystems, with each species playing its role in the delicate balance of underwater life. Schools of sergeant majors and blue tangs moved like living clouds through the water, while a pair of queen angelfish glided regally among the coral branches. Smaller wrasses, gobies and clownfish darted in and out of hiding places, their nervous energy a constant reminder of the ocean's perpetual dance between predator and prey.

Tonight, however, the reef felt different. Most of the fish had retreated deep into the coral formations, and even the normally bold moray eel had withdrawn completely into its cave. Only Neptune remained visible, moving in slow, deliberate circles around the floating form of Dr. Jennifer Parker, as if standing guard over something he couldn't understand but knew was wrong.

How the hell did she get in there? I wondered, not for the first time.

"How could she have gotten in there, Mr. Williams?" I asked. As far as I could tell, there was no way to get around the back.

"There's a service gangway round back," he replied. "If you'll follow me, I'll show you."

He led us to a barely visible door in a black wall some thirty feet to the right of the tank, and through that we followed him into the service area.

"No security cameras back here?" I asked.

He shook his head. "No need for them," he said. "No one's allowed back here. Staff only."

I shook my head. *Really?* I thought. *That makes no sense, but what do I know?*

He walked us forward until we were standing behind what appeared to be a gigantic black box. "This is the back of the tank," he said. "That's the gangway I was telling you about." He pointed upward at a steel walkway some ten feet above our heads.

"And that's the filtration system for this tank," he continued, pointing to two very large, gray-painted MAT drum filters.

"I need to get up there," I said.

"This way," Williams replied, and he led me to the far end

of the tank where a flight of steel steps provided access to the gangway.

I climbed the steps and cautiously stepped on the steel walkway. The top of the tank was now waist high. *Hmm, easy enough to tip someone over,* I thought.

The surface of the water was about six inches below the top of the tank. I could see Neptune swimming close to the surface some twenty feet away and the body of the woman a few feet beyond.

I stood for a moment, then went back down the steps to rejoin Kate.

"What do you think?" Kate asked.

"Access is easy enough," I said. "The walkway puts you right at the edge of the tank. She could have been pushed, or maybe she fell accidentally while trying to help the turtle."

"Or maybe she was already unconscious when she went in," Kate said quietly.

"Yeah, that too," I replied. *What was she even doing here?* I wondered.

Kate's radio crackled, and she answered it. "Gazzara."

"Captain, the CSI team is en route, ETA ten minutes. The medical examiner is coming from Chattanooga General—Doc Sheddon's out of town for a couple weeks."

"Copy that," she said and turned to one of the uniformed officers—a sergeant Millen—who'd followed us into the service area. "Secure the perimeter," she told him, "and don't let anyone else inside until CSI gets here."

Kate then turned to me. "A hospital pathologist instead of Doc," she said, slowly shaking her head. "That's going to complicate things."

"I'm sure it is," I agreed.

"Doc knows how we work," she said. "He understands

what we need and when we need it. And this hospital guy is going to be working out of his comfort zone."

Kate's CSI supervisor Michael Willis arrived fifteen minutes later with his team. Willis was exactly as I remembered him—short, overweight, a completely bald head that seemed to shine under the lights, and thick bushy eyebrows that gave him an owlish appearance. He'd been processing crime scenes since before I joined the force, and despite his eccentric personality, he was thorough and competent.

"Well, this is interesting," Willis said, studying the tank setup. "A dead body, closed environment, controlled access. Going to be a challenge getting everything out without contaminating evidence."

"How long do you need?" Kate asked.

"Six hours minimum. Maybe a lot longer if we find anything unusual in the water samples."

Williams had been standing quietly nearby, still looking shaken. Kate turned to him with her notebook ready.

"Mr. Williams, I need you to walk me through your discovery once more, step by step, and"—she took out her phone and set it to record—"I'm going to record our conversation, if that's all right with you." She looked at him. He nodded. "Out loud, please, Mr. Williams."

"Sure. That's okay," he replied nervously.

"What time did you first notice something was wrong?" she asked.

"It was twelve-fifteen, maybe twelve-twenty," Williams said. "I always check the big exhibits on my midnight rounds. The turtle tank is usually one of my favorite stops—Neptune's such a character, always swimming up to the glass when he sees me."

"But not tonight?"

"No, tonight he was swimming up there, then I saw… her." His voice broke slightly. "I knew she was dead."

"Did you see anyone else in the building tonight? Any staff working late, any maintenance people?"

"Nobody. The building was empty when I started my shift at eleven. I always do a complete walk-through when I arrive."

"What time does the aquarium close?" I asked.

"Five o'clock. The last entry is at five. It can take up to an hour for the last visitor to leave."

"And the staff?" I asked.

"Well, there's maintenance to do, of course, but most are gone by nine."

Kate continued to question him while I observed his body language. He seemed genuinely shaken, but there was something else. Nervousness beyond what you'd expect from someone who'd discovered a body. But then, such things affect people in different ways.

"Mr. Williams," I said, "during the last several months, have you ever had any security issues? Break-ins, vandalism, anyone trying to get into areas they shouldn't?"

Williams glanced at Kate, then back at me. "Who are you exactly?"

"I'm a private investigator," I said. "I'm here at Captain Gazzara's invitation."

"Oh, right. Well then…" he seemed a little less nervous. Maybe it was me that was intimidating him. I can't think why. I glanced down at Samson. He was standing close to Kate, and he seemed happy enough with the man. *If he's good enough for Sammy,* I thought. *He's good enough for me.*

"Well, yes," he continued, "we've had a few incidents over the years. Mostly teenagers trying to get in after hours, that sort of thing. But nothing serious. The security system is pretty good."

"What about the service areas?" I asked. "How many people have access to that walkway?" I glanced up at it.

"Maybe a dozen staff members," he replied. "Maintenance, research staff, senior aquarists. Management."

"I'll need a list of all the employees and everyone with access," Kate said, "and I'll need to know who's been in and out of the building during the last forty-eight hours."

He blew out through his lips. "Wow. You'll have to see HR for the employees and volunteers. As for the rest, you'll have to see Sam for that, Sam Carter, my boss. He keeps the logs, but he doesn't get in 'till eight."

The medical examiner turned out not to be a guy at all. Dr. Patricia Hensley, the pathologist from Chattanooga General Hospital, arrived just as Willis was setting up his equipment. She was a woman in her mid-forties, professionally dressed despite the early hour, carrying the standard medical examiner's kit. She looked uncomfortable in the aquarium setting.

"Are you Captain Gazzara?" she asked.

"I am," she replied. "And you're the pathologist, correct?"

"I'm Dr. Hensley," she replied. "I understand you have a drowning victim?"

"We have a body," Kate replied. "As to the cause of death, we're hoping you'll provide that. The victim is up there, in the tank." She half-turned and pointed. "But CSI needs to document everything before we can remove the body."

Dr. Hensley peered through the acrylic glass, frowning. "This is highly unusual. How long before we can get her out? I'll need to examine the body, and I'll need to take water samples to determine if there are any foreign substances in the tank."

"My CSI supervisor, Lieutenant Mike Willis, is handling the water analysis," Kate said. "How long will it take you to determine cause and time of death once you can examine the victim?"

"Preliminary examination tonight, full autopsy tomorrow. I should have initial results by Monday morning."

I watched Dr. Hensley's face as she studied the scene. She was clearly out of her element, more accustomed to hospital deaths and more traditional crime scenes than aquarium exhibits, which could be a problem if the case turned complicated.

"Hmm, I was hoping you could give us a rough estimate now," Kate began. "Dr Sheddon—"

"Yes, I know all about Dr. Sheddon," she said, cutting her off. "I'll do what I can, but no promises."

"Come find me when you're done," Kate said, shortly, then turned and walked away. I smiled at Hensley and then followed her.

"I'm not sure about her," Kate said, obviously peeved at being interrupted.

Aquarium board member Victoria Ashcroft arrived next, just as the medical team was preparing to remove the body from the tank. Victoria was an imposing woman in her mid-fifties, tall, silver hair perfectly styled, wearing an expensive coat over what appeared to be evening wear. Even at three in the morning, she looked like she'd just stepped out of a boardroom.

"Captain Gazzara," Victoria said, approaching with the confidence of someone accustomed to being in charge. "I came as soon as I heard. This is absolutely tragic."

"Ma'am, this is an active crime scene," Kate replied. "I must ask you to stay behind the perimeter tape."

"Of course. I simply wanted to offer any assistance the aquarium can provide. This facility serves thousands of families and children each month. We're deeply concerned about how this tragedy might affect our reputation and our educational mission."

I noted how quickly Victoria had shifted from expressing sympathy to managing potential damage to the aquarium's image. She was already thinking three steps ahead, planning crisis management before we'd even determined what had happened.

"We'll need to speak with you about the victim once we've formally identified her," Kate said. "She's been identified by the security guard as Dr. Jennifer Parker. I understand she worked here and at UTC."

Victoria's composed expression flickered for just a moment—surprise, or perhaps something else—before she regained her professional demeanor.

"Dr. Parker? Oh dear God, that's terrible," she said, her hand moving to her throat. "Yes, she's been working with our research team on a water quality project. She's with the environmental toxicology department at UTC. This is just... I can't believe she's dead."

Victoria paused, seeming to collect herself. "Captain, I have to ask—was this an accident? Could she have fallen into the tank somehow?"

"That's still to be determined," Kate replied. "When did you last see Dr. Parker?"

"Earlier this week, I think. Tuesday, maybe Wednesday. She was here for a project meeting with our marine biology staff. She seemed fine; very focused on her research."

"What kind of research was she conducting?" Kate asked.

"Water quality assessments, microplastics in the river

system. You do know this aquarium's focus is on the Tennessee River, don't you? Most of the tanks here represent that environment. Hers was important environmental work. She was very passionate about it." Victoria glanced toward the tank, then back at Kate. "Captain, I hope you understand how devastating this could be for the aquarium's reputation. If word gets out that someone died here..."

The shift from expressing grief to protecting the institution's image was swift and telling.

Kate's expression didn't change, but I could see the slight tightening around her eyes that indicated irritation. "Ma'am, our priority is to determine exactly what happened here, not managing public relations."

"Of course, Captain," she replied coldly. "I understand completely."

Dr. Wiley Jones, one of the aquarium's marine biologists, arrived shortly after Victoria. He was a small, nervous man in his early forties with thinning dark hair and thick glasses. Unlike Victoria's composed demeanor, Jones appeared genuinely distraught.

"My God," Jones whispered, staring at the tank. "Is that... is that Dr. Parker?"

Kate immediately turned and focused on him. "You know the victim?"

"If it's who I think it is, yes. Dr. Jennifer Parker. She's a researcher at UTC, environmental toxicology. She's been working with us on a water quality project."

"Yes, I know," Kate said. "I've already spoken to Mrs. Ashcroft. When did you last see Dr. Parker?"

Jones ran his hands through his hair nervously. "Ah, yes," he muttered, then looked at Kate and said, "Yesterday evening, around six o'clock. She said she wanted to stay and finish some tests. She'd been working on something urgent—research funded by a private foundation about pollution; microplastics in the Tennessee River system."

I exchanged glances with Kate. Environmental research could generate surprising controversies, especially when findings threatened established interests.

"Dr. Jones," Kate said, "I'll need you to stay available for questioning. Don't leave town without contacting us first."

"Am I a suspect?" Jones asked, his voice rising slightly.

"At this point, everyone who had contact with Dr. Parker in the last few days is a person of interest. That's standard procedure. Now, if you'll excuse us…"

He nodded and turned away.

"I don't think he likes Ashcroft," I said.

"She has her priorities wrong," Kate replied. "I wouldn't want to work for her, would you?"

Dr. Hensley completed her preliminary examination of Dr. Parker's body on a portable gurney that Willis had set up near the tank. She worked methodically, taking photographs and making notes while Kate and I watched from a respectful distance.

"Well?" Kate asked when Hensley finally looked up from her clipboard.

"This is… very unusual," Dr. Hensley said, frowning at her notes. "I can't determine cause of death definitively without a full autopsy, but there are some significant anomalies."

"What anomalies?" Kate asked, frowning.

"The victim's pupils are extremely dilated, and the muscle rigidity is inconsistent with typical drowning victims. The body positioning suggests she may have been paralyzed before entering the water. And there are signs of cyanosis, the bluish discoloration of the skin, lips, fingers, and toenails that indicate a lack of oxygen due to respiratory failure."

I leaned forward. "You're saying she was paralyzed?"

"I'm sorry," she said. "Who are you?"

"Harry Starke," Kate said. "He's with me. Please continue, Doctor."

"Paralyzed? Yes! That's what the external signs suggest. The facial expression and body posture indicate severe muscle paralysis. If I had to guess, I'd say she was poisoned with some kind of neurotoxin."

"So she didn't just fall in and drown?" Kate asked.

"Highly unlikely," Hensley replied. "I won't know for certain until I can perform the full autopsy and run toxicology tests, but the external examination suggests poisoning."

"Time of death?" Kate asked.

"Based on body temperature and rigor mortis, I'd estimate between nine and ten-thirty PM last night."

"What kind of poison could cause this?" I asked.

"Several possibilities. Some marine toxins, certain pharmaceuticals, various plant-based neurotoxins. I'll need lab work to identify the specific agent."

Dr. Hensley packed up her equipment. "Captain, based on what I can observe here, it looks like the victim was murdered."

Geez, I thought as we left her to it with her promise to call Kate when she'd finished the autopsy.

The rest of the crime scene processing took another four hours. By the time we left the aquarium, dawn was breaking over the Tennessee River, painting the sky in shades of orange and pink that reminded me uncomfortably of the Hunter's Moon that had started this whole night.

At home, I found Amanda already up and in the kitchen,

drinking coffee and scrolling through the early morning news reports on her phone. My wife's journalist instincts had kicked in the moment she heard about the incident at the aquarium.

"Strange case?" Amanda asked, looking up from her phone.

"Strange doesn't begin to cover it," I replied, pouring myself coffee. "A marine biologist-environmentalist found dead in a sea turtle tank. Almost certainly murder. Geez, I've been up all night. I need coffee. Jade still asleep?"

Amanda nodded, set down her phone and studied my face. After almost ten years of marriage, she could read my expressions as well as Kate could read crime scenes.

"You don't think it could have been an accident?"

"No," I said. "I don't think it's an accident."

The Hunter's Moon had long been set behind the mountains when I sat down at my desk in my home office to review my mental notes. One thing I was certain of was that Dr. Jennifer Parker's death was going to be complicated: environmental research, nervous colleagues, sophisticated security systems, and an inquisitive sea turtle. Yes, it was going to be complicated. But it was also interesting, at least to me. I'd always been a sucker for an impossible crime, and this one had all the makings.

Kate had already mentioned she was going to need my help. The question was, whether Chief Johnston would authorize my involvement or whether Kate would have to work this case with her regular team.

Either way, I suspected the Hunter's Moon had brought us more than just a restless night.

2

_____

Deep Waters

Monday Morning

I WAS TAKING IT EASY WHEN MY PHONE RANG AT NINE-THIRTY the next morning, Monday. I glanced at the screen. It was Kate, and I knew she hadn't called to chat about weekend plans.

"Please tell me you have good news about Dr. Parker," I said, skipping the pleasantries.

"Dr. Hensley called me just after six Sunday evening with the preliminary autopsy results. I didn't want to disturb you on a Sunday, so I waited 'till this morning to call you," Kate replied. "She confirmed that Dr. Parker was murdered. She found an injection site on the victim's neck, right behind the left ear. A small puncture wound, easily missed in the preliminary examination."

"What was it?" I asked. "Was she able to say?"

"Yep, she called me with the results of the tox screen just a few minutes ago. It was Tetrodotoxin. It comes from puffer-fish, apparently. Causes complete paralysis while leaving the victim conscious. She would have been awake but unable to move or call for help when she went into the water."

"Geez," I muttered. "That's a particularly nasty way to kill someone. Any idea where the killer might have gotten something like that?"

"That's what we need to find out. But first, I need to run something by Chief Johnston. Can you meet me at the station in an hour? I want to get you officially brought on board, if he'll go for it."

"I'll be there."

An hour later, I was sitting in Chief Wesley Johnston's office with Kate and Samson while she made her case for bringing me in as a consultant. Johnston was a big man who filled his chair as if it had been custom built for him. His completely bald head gleamed under the fluorescent lights, and his white mustache would have made Hulk Hogan proud. He'd been running the Chattanooga Police Department for almost thirty years, and he had the kind of presence that made even seasoned cops straighten their shoulders.

"Captain Gazzara tells me this aquarium case has some unusual elements," Johnston said, studying me across his desk. "Marine toxins, sophisticated security, environmental research angles. Not your typical homicide."

"No, sir, it's not," I replied.

Johnston leaned back in his chair. "And you think your particular expertise would be valuable here?"

"Come on, Chief," I replied. "You know me. Hell, I worked for you for eight years, and who did you turn to—"

"All right," he snapped, cutting me off. "That's enough."

Johnston was quiet for a moment, then nodded. "All right, Harry. Same arrangement as usual—consultant status, no pay." He looked at Kate. "And he reports only to you. And I want regular updates, and if this case generates political pressure, we may need to reassess."

"Understood, Chief."

"And Harry," Johnston said, fixing me with a stern look, "I know you have a tendency to bend the rules when it suits you. This is a high-profile case at a major tourist attraction. Everything by the book. Understood?"

I grinned at him. "Yes, sir."

"Go on, get out of here, both of you," he said, unable to hide a rare, though small, smile.

Twenty minutes later, Kate and I, with Samson in the back seat, were driving toward the University of Tennessee at Chattanooga campus. Our thinking was that Dr. Parker's colleagues might be able to provide insights into her research and any threats she might have faced.

"What did Dr. Hensley say about the timing?" I asked as Kate navigated through the morning traffic.

"No change. Between nine and ten-thirty PM Saturday night," Kate replied. "She seemed pretty confident."

"I would damn well hope so," I said as I made a mental note of the timeframe. If the timeline held up, it would help narrow down suspects and alibis.

"Did she say where someone might get tetrodotoxin?" I asked.

"She did. She said it's found in pufferfish, the blue-ringed octopus, some newts and frogs, and that it could be extracted in a laboratory by anyone with the knowledge and equipment."

"So we're looking for someone with access to marine specimens and the expertise to extract and concentrate the toxin," I said.

"Yep, and I'd say there's plenty of those around at the aquarium and UTC."

Kate had tracked down Dr. Parker's closest colleague through the university directory. The UTC campus was quiet on Monday morning, but Dr. Sally Howard had agreed to meet us at the Environmental Sciences building, where we found her waiting for us in the lobby.

She was an attractive woman in her late thirties, with shoulder-length auburn hair and intelligent green eyes that showed signs of recent crying. She wore jeans and a UTC sweatshirt, and she looked like she hadn't slept all weekend.

"Captain Gazzara?" she asked, approaching us with her hand extended and her eyes on Samson. I couldn't blame her. He's a formidable-looking creature, especially when wearing his official K-9 harness and badge.

"I'm Sally Howard, Marine Biology department. I am so upset. I still can't believe Jennifer's gone. D'you know who murdered her?"

"Thank you for meeting with us, Dr. Howard," Kate said, shaking her hand. "This is my colleague, Harry Starke. We're very sorry for your loss, but no. As yet, we have no suspects, but it's very early in the investigation and we *will* find the person who did this."

"Please call me Sally," she said, then looked at me and offered me her hand. "Mr. Starke? I've heard of you; you're a private investigator. I've seen you on TV, haven't I?"

"Sometimes," I replied, shaking her hand. "I'm sorry we have to meet under these circumstances, Sally."

She led us to a small conference room on the second floor. *Hmm, interesting,* I thought as I looked around. The walls were covered with charts showing river ecosystems and marine food chains, and the windows looked out over the Tennessee River in the distance.

"Jennifer and I worked closely together," Sally said, settling into a chair across from us. "Her research complemented my marine biology work. We often collaborated on projects involving aquatic ecosystems."

Kate opened her notebook, set her phone to record, then asked for her permission to record the interview, then said, "Let's begin with the obvious. Do you know anyone who might have wanted to harm Dr. Parker? "

She paused for a moment, then said, "No one. I can't think of anyone. She was a sweet person. Everyone loved her."

I frowned at that. There was something about her body language that didn't seem quite right as she said it. I leaned back in my chair, arms folded, watching her.

"How well did you know Dr. Parker?" Kate asked.

"Very well," she replied. "As I said, we were colleagues of sorts. Our projects often overlapped."

"About her work?" Kate said. "Can you tell us about Dr. Parker's current research? We understand she was working on something involving the Tennessee River."

"It's quite simple," she replied. "She was investigating pollution and the illegal disposal of chemical and industrial waste in the river system. The research was funded by the Ashcroft Environmental Research Initiative. Jennifer had been working on it for about six months."

"Ashcroft," I said. "As in Victoria Ashcroft from the aquarium board?"

"Yes, that's right. Jennifer mentioned that the funding came through the aquarium's connections, but she worked directly with the foundation."

Kate made notes while I continued to study Sally's body language. She seemed genuinely grief-stricken, but there was something else in her expression. Something that looked almost like anger beneath the sadness.

"Sally," Kate said gently, "was your relationship with Dr. Parker purely professional?"

Sally's composure wavered for a moment, and she looked down at her hands. "No. Jennifer and I... we were... lovers. We'd been together for almost two years. We tried to keep it private because of university policies about relationships between colleagues."

"I'm sorry," Kate said. "That must make this even more difficult."

Sally wiped her eyes with a tissue. "Jennifer was brilliant, passionate about her work. She genuinely believed she could make a difference in protecting the river ecosystem. She'd been getting more and more concerned about what she was finding in her research."

"What kind of concerns?" I asked.

"The contamination levels were much higher than expected, and the patterns suggested deliberate dumping rather than accidental runoff," she replied. "Jennifer said the chemical signatures pointed to industrial waste, possibly from multiple sources."

Kate looked up from her notes. "Did she mention any specific companies or locations?"

"She was being careful about making accusations without solid proof. But she'd identified several areas where the contamination was most concentrated. She spent a lot of time taking samples around the Raccoon Mountain area and some of the smaller creeks that feed into the main river."

"Did Dr. Parker express any concerns about her safety?"

Kate asked. "Any indication that someone might want to stop her research?"

I watched as Sally's expression darkened. She stared at her hands for several seconds before answering.

"About two weeks ago, she said she felt like she was being watched. She thought someone had been following her when she went out to collect samples. I told her she was being paranoid, but now..." She trailed off, shaking her head.

So that's it, I thought.

"Did she say she suspected anyone, or anything about confronting anyone?" I asked. "Someone connected to the companies she suspected might be responsible for the contamination?"

"That's why Jennifer had reached out to Michael Drake," Sally continued. "He's an investigative journalist who specializes in environmental crimes. He lives on a houseboat at Chickamauga Marina and has been investigating river pollution throughout the Southeast for years. Jennifer thought that between them they could force the authorities to take action against whoever was responsible for the illegal dumping."

"Was there anything else?" I asked. "Anyone else?"

Sally hesitated, then nodded. "Saturday afternoon," she replied, nodding. "She called me around four o'clock. She was upset, angry. She said she'd discovered something that proved her suspicions about the dumping, and she was going to confront the person responsible."

"Did she say who?" Kate asked.

"Yes, Victoria Ashcroft. Said she was going to meet her at the aquarium and demand an explanation. I tried to talk her out of it. I told her to stay away from Victoria and take whatever it was she'd found to the EPA or the police. But Jennifer was... she could be stubborn when she thought she was right. She called again later to say she was on her way."

Kate and I exchanged glances. If Jennifer Parker had confronted Victoria Ashcroft on Saturday night, that would place Victoria at the scene around the time of the murder.

"What time was that phone call?" I asked.

"Around eight o'clock Saturday night, give or take a few minutes. Jennifer said she was going to drive to the aquarium and wait for Victoria to show up."

"And that was the last time you spoke with her?" Kate asked.

Sally nodded, fresh tears forming in her eyes. "I should have gone with her. Or insisted she wait until Monday and handle it through official channels. If only I'd been there..."

"Dr. Howard," Kate said firmly, "this is not your fault. Dr. Parker was the victim of a premeditated murder. The person responsible is the only one to blame."

"Getting back to Michael Drake," I said. "When were they supposed to meet?"

"Saturday night. Jennifer said if her confrontation with Victoria went badly, she wanted to share all her findings with Drake so he could publish the story and expose what's been happening to the Tennessee River."

I leaned forward. "Sally, based on your knowledge of marine biology, how difficult would it be for someone to obtain and prepare tetrodotoxin?"

She looked puzzled. "Tetrodotoxin? That's the neurotoxin from pufferfish. Why do you ask?"

"Because, according to the pathologist, that's probably what killed Dr. Parker."

Sally's face went pale. "Oh God. Jennifer was poisoned with tetrodotoxin?"

"You're familiar with it?" Kate asked.

"Of course I am. It's one of the most potent neurotoxins in nature. Complete paralysis while leaving the victim conscious and aware. It's... it's a horrible way to die." She shuddered. "Anyone with advanced marine biology training would know about it, and it could be extracted from pufferfish specimens with the right laboratory equipment."

"How many people would have that kind of knowledge and access?" I asked.

"In this area? Maybe a dozen marine biologists, some research technicians, possibly some aquarium staff; those with advanced training. It's not common knowledge, but it's not exactly a secret either."

"Sally," Kate said, "you said Jennifer was going to confront Victoria Ashcroft. How well do you know Victoria?"

Sally's expression darkened slightly. "I've met her a few times at university functions and aquarium events. She's on several boards around town, always presenting herself as this great environmental advocate." There was a bitter edge to her voice. "Jennifer had to work with her because of the research funding."

"What was your impression of her?" I asked.

"Polished, controlling, very concerned about appearances. She struck me as someone who was more interested in the public relations value of environmental work than actually protecting the environment." Sally paused, then added, "Jennifer found her frustrating to deal with."

"In what way?" Kate asked.

"Victoria always wanted to control the narrative around Jennifer's research. She'd make suggestions about which areas to focus on. Jennifer felt like Victoria was trying to steer the research away from certain findings."

Kate leaned forward. "What kind of findings?"

"The worst contamination areas. Jennifer said Victoria always had explanations for why those particular sites weren't worth investigating further, or why the results might be misleading."

I exchanged a glance with Kate. "Sally, do you think Victoria Ashcroft could have killed Jennifer?"

Sally was quiet for a long moment, her hands clasped tightly in her lap. When she finally spoke, her voice was barely above a whisper.

"A week ago, I would have said absolutely not. But now, knowing what Jennifer discovered, knowing she was going to confront Victoria about the dumping..." She looked up at us, her eyes filled with pain and anger. "If Victoria was involved in poisoning the river, if she stood to lose millions of dollars or face criminal charges because of Jennifer's research, then yes. I think she could have killed her."

"But does she have the knowledge and expertise to produce the neurotoxin?" Kate asked.

Sally shook her head slowly. "Not directly. Victoria has a business background, not scientific training. She wouldn't know how to extract and purify tetrodotoxin herself." She paused, then continued thoughtfully, "But she has connections to people who would. The aquarium employs several marine biologists, and through her various environmental foundations, she works with researchers from multiple universities. She could easily have had someone else prepare it for her."

"Anyone specific come to mind?" I asked.

"Well, there's Dr. Jones at the aquarium. He has the expertise. And she funds research at several institutions. She'd have access to people with the necessary knowledge and laboratory facilities." Sally's voice grew harder. "Victoria Ashcroft is the type of person who gets other people to do her dirty work while keeping her own hands clean."

Kate closed her notebook. "Dr. Howard, we'll need a list of everyone Dr. Parker worked with, both here at the university and at the aquarium. We'll also need copies of her research files and any correspondence about the river contamination project."

"Of course. I'll get you everything I can access. I have a key to Jennifer's office... because we shared some equipment."

"You do? Then perhaps we could take a look at her office. D'you mind?"

"Of course," Sally replied immediately. "It's just down the hall from mine." She stood up, wiping her eyes. "I'll show you everything she was working on."

We spent the next hour going through Jennifer's office with Sally's help. Her research was meticulous and extensive, with detailed maps of sample locations, water quality measurements, and chemical analysis reports spread across her desk and pinned to a large corkboard. The data painted a disturbing picture of systematic pollution in several specific areas of the Tennessee River system, particularly around the creek systems west of Raccoon Mountain. Sally moved through the office with familiar ease, explaining Jennifer's filing system and pointing out the most significant findings. She was able to interpret the data quickly, and I noticed she paid particular attention to the evidence that pointed toward deliberate environmental crimes. Watching her work, it was clear that Sally understood the implications of Jennifer's research better than anyone—and that knowledge, I realized, made her a valuable ally in our investigation.

"Look at this," I said, pointing to a map covered with red

markers. "She highlighted these areas clustered around the creek system west of Raccoon Mountain. And these chemical signatures—they're consistent with industrial solvents and heavy metals."

Kate studied the data. "She was building a case for illegal dumping. This could have cost someone millions in cleanup costs and criminal liability."

"Sally," I said, "did Jennifer ever mention specific time frames for when these dumping incidents might have occurred?"

"She thought they were ongoing," Sally replied. "The freshest contamination suggested dumps within the last few months, maybe even weeks. She said whoever was doing it had detailed knowledge of the water flow patterns and the Chickamauga dam release schedules."

"That suggests coordination with someone who understands the river system," Kate said.

We left the university with boxes of Dr. Parker's research and a growing understanding of why she might have been killed. Someone was systematically poisoning the Tennessee River, and, by the look of it, she'd gathered enough evidence to expose them.

As we drove back toward downtown, Kate's phone rang. She answered on speaker.

"Captain Gazzara."

"Kate, it's Tim. I've been analyzing the security footage from the aquarium, and I found something interesting."

"What kind of something?"

"The system was definitely hacked. Professional job, too. Someone disabled specific cameras while leaving others operational, creating blind spots that would allow access to the service areas behind the Neptune exhibit."

"Any idea who might have that kind of technical expertise?"

"I'm working on it," he replied. "But here's the thing: the hack was initiated from outside the building, early Saturday evening. Whoever did this planned it in advance."

Kate and I looked at each other. The timeline was starting to come together. Dr. Parker calls Sally on Saturday afternoon and evening about confronting Victoria. The aquarium's security system gets hacked early evening. Dr. Parker turns up dead Saturday night.

"Tim, I need you to check something else for me, please," Kate said. "See if you can find any connection between Victoria Ashcroft and companies that might be involved in river dumping operations."

"I'm on it."

Tim is my IT expert, computer geek, whatever. He's been with me since before he dropped out of college when he was seventeen, just one small step ahead of the law. Yeah, he was a hacker, and still is when he needs to be. He's also the best at what he does, bar none. I'd sent him copies of the security footage.

"What's your read of Dr. Howard?" I asked Kate.

"Grieving, angry, wants justice for her girlfriend," she replied. "She's hiding something, though. I could see it in her eyes when we talked about the confrontation with Victoria."

"What kind of something?"

"I'm not sure yet. Maybe just guilt about not stopping Jennifer from going to the aquarium alone. Or maybe she knows more about the environmental crimes than she's letting on."

"She certainly has the scientific knowledge to understand tetrodotoxin," I said.

"So do a lot of other people, apparently. We need to focus on who had motive, means, and opportunity."

As we pulled into the police department parking lot, Kate's phone rang again. This time it was Dr. Hensley.

"Captain, I have the complete toxicology results. The tetrodotoxin concentration was extremely high. Whoever administered it knew exactly what he or she was doing. This wasn't an accident or an amateur attempt."

"Anything else?"

"The injection was administered with precision. A small needle, probably an insulin syringe, inserted just behind the left ear at an angle that would ensure rapid absorption into the bloodstream."

After Dr. Hensley hung up, Kate and I sat in her car for a moment, processing the information.

"So we're looking for someone with scientific knowledge who knew about Dr. Parker's plans to confront Victoria," Kate said.

"Someone who could hack security systems, and obtain and prepare tetrodotoxin, and knew enough about anatomy to administer it effectively," I added.

"The question is whether Victoria Ashcroft fits that profile, or whether it was someone else who wanted Dr. Parker dead."

As we walked into the police department, my gut was telling me we were dealing with something much more complex than a simple murder. And somewhere out there, someone was continuing to poison the Tennessee River while we tried to piece together the truth about Dr. Jennifer Parker's death.

3

Dangerous Currents

Tuesday/Wednesday

TUESDAY MORNING BROUGHT NO RELIEF FROM THE COMPLEXITY of Dr. Parker's murder. I was in my home office at seven AM, reviewing the environmental research files we'd collected from Jennifer Parker's UTC office, when Kate called.

"We've got a problem," she said after the usual pleasantries. "I just got off the phone with Chief Johnston. He's had three calls already this morning from city council members asking why we're 'harassing' Victoria Ashcroft."

"Harassing?" I said, setting down the water quality report I'd been studying. "We haven't even talked to her yet. All we did was ask her a few questions at the crime scene."

"Apparently, someone told them we were treating her as a suspect in the aquarium murder. According to Councilman

Bradley, we're 'wasting taxpayer money pursuing a vendetta against one of Chattanooga's most respected citizens.'"

I could hear the frustration in Kate's voice. Political interference was always a complication in high-profile cases, but this seemed unusually aggressive for such an early stage of the investigation.

"Who's coordinating the pushback?" I asked.

"That's what I want to know. Johnston wants to see us in his office at nine. He sounded like someone had been working on him all night."

An hour later, Kate and I along with Samson were sitting across from Chief Johnston's desk while he read from what appeared to be carefully prepared talking points. His usual confidence seemed strained, and I noticed he avoided making direct eye contact with either of us.

"Mrs. Ashcroft has been a pillar of this community for over twenty years," Johnston said, his tone suggesting he wasn't entirely comfortable with the words. "She serves on the hospital board, the environmental foundation board, the chamber of commerce, and has contributed over half a million dollars to local charities in the past five years alone. She has never had so much as a parking ticket."

"Chief," Kate said carefully, "we're following the evidence. Dr. Parker called her girlfriend, Dr. Sally Howard—they're… together, or perhaps I should say they were—Saturday evening and specifically said she was going to confront Victoria Ashcroft about environmental crimes. Six hours later, Parker's dead; the murder weapon, an exotic poison."

Johnston shifted uncomfortably in his chair. "That's circumstantial at best, Captain. And Mrs. Ashcroft has a solid alibi for Saturday evening. She was at the Riverside Hospital Foundation gala from seven until just after eleven. Over two hundred witnesses saw her there throughout the evening, plus there are photographs, security footage of her arrival and departure, and dozens of people who spoke with her during the event."

I made careful mental notes of the timeframe. If Dr. Hensley's time of death estimate was accurate—nine to ten-thirty PM—Victoria's alibi covered the critical period perfectly. *Hmm, perhaps too perfect*, I thought.

"Chief, what about the environmental crimes Parker was investigating?" I asked. "The illegal dumping, the chemical contamination, the systematic poisoning of the river system? Shouldn't we be following up on those connections?"

Johnston's expression hardened, and for the first time during our meeting, he looked directly at me. "Harry, your job —both of your jobs—is to find Dr. Parker's killer, not to investigate every environmental complaint in Hamilton County. The EPA handles pollution issues. The Tennessee Department of Environment and Conservation handles water quality. We handle murders. Got it?"

"But the two are obviously connected," Kate insisted. "Parker was killed because of what she discovered about the illegal dumping. You can't separate the environmental crimes from the homicide."

"Maybe they are connected, maybe they aren't," Johnston replied. "But I don't want this department accused of conducting a fishing expedition against prominent citizens based on speculation and circumstantial evidence. You stick to the murder, you find the killer using proper police procedures, and you let other agencies handle their own jurisdictions."

His tone had the finality of an order, not a suggestion. Someone had definitely gotten to him.

"What if the environmental crimes are the motive for the murder?" I asked.

"Then you prove it with evidence, not accusations. And you do it without harassing people who have alibis and community standing." Johnston stood up, clearly ending the meeting. "Is that understood?"

"Yes, sir," Kate said. She sounded thoroughly frustrated.

As we left Johnston's office, Kate shook her head grimly. "Someone got to him. That wasn't the chief I know. Johnston usually has a spine when it comes to political pressure."

"Victoria Ashcroft has influence," I said. "Money talks, especially in a city this size. But this level of coordination suggests something more organized than just one wealthy woman making phone calls."

"Yeah, but Johnston's been chief for almost three decades," Kate replied. "He's weathered political storms before. This feels different, more intense."

"Maybe because the stakes are higher than we realize," I said. "If Ashcroft Chemical has been dumping illegally for decades, we're talking about millions in cleanup costs, criminal liability, and federal charges. That's worth fighting for."

We spent the rest of Tuesday morning trying to track down potential sources of tetrodotoxin, despite the political constraints Johnston had placed on us. Kate contacted marine biology departments at regional universities while I called aquariums, research facilities, and private laboratories that might have access to pufferfish specimens.

The story was remarkably consistent everywhere—tetrodotoxin was well known among marine biologists as one of nature's most potent neurotoxins. It was potentially lethal in tiny doses, could be extracted from pufferfish specimens with the right equipment and knowledge, and was used in legitimate research into nerve function and paralysis.

What troubled me, though, was discovering how many people had access to both the knowledge and the means to get it. The University of Tennessee had a marine science program with active research projects. Vanderbilt University's biology department had several researchers working with marine toxins. Three community colleges in the region offered marine biology courses with laboratory components. The Tennessee Aquarium employed multiple marine biologists and research technicians. And at least three private research companies in the Southeast specialized in marine biotechnology. And we hadn't even contacted UTK, Georgia Tech, or Alabama University. It was a proverbial needle in the haystack problem.

"It's not exactly a smoking gun," Kate said after we'd compiled our list of over forty potential suspects. "Half of the marine biology community in Tennessee and North Georgia could have prepared the toxin that killed Dr. Parker."

"But not everyone had access to her research, and knew about her plans to confront Victoria, or felt threatened enough by her discoveries to commit murder," I replied. "We need to focus on people who had motive, means, and opportunity—not just the technical capability."

"The problem is proving motive when we're not supposed to investigate the environmental crimes that would provide it," Kate said.

Kate's phone rang while we were reviewing our suspect list. She answered it on speaker.

"Captain Gazzara."

"Kate, this is Amanda. I've been doing some research on

the Ashcroft family history like you asked, and I found something very interesting." Kate put the phone on speaker.

Amanda, aside from being my wife, is a senior news anchor at Channel 7 and has a journalist's instincts for investigation that rivals most detectives. After our nine o'clock interview with the chief, I'd called her and asked her to use her media connections to look into the Ashcroft family's business background, and search for patterns that might explain Dr. Parker's murder and the political pressure we were facing. If we couldn't do the digging, there was nothing said Amanda couldn't do it for us.

"What kind of something?" Kate asked.

"Victoria's father, William Ashcroft, died fifteen years ago under what I would call highly suspicious circumstances. He was found dead in his home office on a Sunday morning, apparently from a massive heart attack. He was only sixty-two years old, in good health, with no history of heart problems."

"That's not necessarily suspicious," I said. "Heart attacks can strike anyone."

"True, but here's where it gets interesting," Amanda continued. "According to my sources at the EPA, William Ashcroft had contacted federal investigators three weeks before his death. He'd scheduled a meeting to discuss what he called 'serious environmental violations' at Ashcroft Chemical. He was planning to provide documentation of illegal waste disposal practices going back twenty years."

Kate and I exchanged a glance. "What happened at that meeting?" Kate asked.

"It never took place. Ashcroft died three days before his scheduled appointment with the EPA investigators. And here's the really suspicious part: the family insisted on immediate cremation, within twenty-four hours of his death, before anyone could request an independent autopsy or toxicology examination."

"Who made that decision?" I asked.

"Victoria Ashcroft, as executor of her father's estate. She had the authority to authorize cremation, and she exercised it immediately. The family funeral director later said he'd never seen anyone push for such rapid cremation of a family member."

"So if William Ashcroft was murdered to prevent him from exposing the company's environmental crimes, the evidence literally went up in smoke," Kate said.

"Exactly. But here's the pattern that really caught my attention," Amanda said. "After William Ashcroft's death, Victoria took over the company and immediately implemented what appeared to be comprehensive environmental reforms. On paper, Ashcroft Chemical became a model corporate citizen. They hired environmental consultants, established new waste disposal protocols, and even started funding environmental research projects throughout the region."

"Like the Ashcroft Environmental Research Initiative that was paying for Dr. Parker's work," I said.

"Precisely. It's almost as if Victoria was trying to buy environmental credibility after her father's death, establishing a public image as someone who cared about protecting the environment."

"While secretly continuing the illegal dumping operations her father had planned to expose," Kate added.

"That's my theory," Amanda said. "The public environmental initiatives were a cover for continuing the crimes that had made the company profitable for decades."

After Amanda hung up, Kate and I sat in her office

processing the implications. The pattern was becoming clearer and more disturbing. Victoria Ashcroft had potentially inherited not just a chemical company, but a legacy of environmental crimes and a willingness to commit murder to protect them. If her father had been killed to prevent him from exposing illegal dumping operations, Victoria would understand exactly how dangerous environmental investigators could be to the family business.

"We need to talk to Michael Drake," I said. "If he was supposed to meet with Dr. Parker Saturday night, he might know something. And he's been investigating Ashcroft Chemical for years. He might have information we can't get through official channels."

"Especially with Johnston limiting our scope," she agreed.

I looked at my watch. It was almost noon. "Now's a good time. Do we have his number?"

We didn't, so I called Tim and two minutes later, we did, and Kate called him. The phone rang four times and then went to voicemail.

Kate hung up and looked at me. I, in turn, looked at her. I didn't have a good feeling about it and, by the look on her face, neither did she.

"My car," she said as she grabbed her jacket and then hooked Sammy up.

Five minutes later we were in her unmarked SUV, lights flashing, on our way to the Chickamauga Marina, where Drake kept his houseboat, a converted forty-foot cabin cruiser that served as both his home and floating office. Samson rode in the back seat, alert and watching the surroundings as we navigated through the marina parking area. It was now Tuesday afternoon, and the marina was quiet, with most of the recreational boats either in storage or out on the water.

We parked the car and walked to Drake's slip, but as we approached, something felt wrong. The houseboat was tied up properly, but there were no lights visible through the windows despite the overcast afternoon. More troubling was the smell—an acrid odor of burnt plastic and chemicals. Samson stopped, sat down, jerking Kate to a stop, his hackles raised. He barked once, a loud, deep warning.

"Got it, Sammy," Kate said, turning to look at him. "Come on, boy." He immediately rose to his feet and joined her, pacing restlessly beside her, clearly agitated by something he sensed we couldn't yet identify.

"Can you smell that, Harry?" she asked, wrinkling her nose. "Sammy's right. It smells... really nasty." She reached for her radio while keeping one hand on Samson's harness to hold him back.

"Something's burning," I agreed, pulling out my phone. "And look at the windows—they're fogged up on the inside."

Kate called for backup and the fire department while I approached the houseboat's main cabin door. Samson stayed close to Kate but continued showing signs of distress, whining softly and pawing at the dock as if trying to alert us to the danger. The closer I got, the stronger the smell became, but now it was accompanied by a faint but ominous beeping sound that I recognized as a smoke or gas detector alarm.

"Drake!" I called out, knocking loudly on the door. "Michael Drake! Chattanooga Police!"

No response. The beeping continued, weak and intermittent, as if the detector's battery was dying.

"We're going in," Kate said as the fire department sirens became audible in the distance.

I kicked in the cabin door, and we were immediately hit by a wave of hot, chemically laden air that made our eyes water.

Kate covered her nose and mouth with her jacket while keeping Samson back from the toxic atmosphere. The big German Shepherd was clearly agitated. I squinted through the haze, trying to locate the source of the problem. I had my nose covered with the sleeve of my jacket. My eyes were watering, blinking as the toxic smoke billowed out the door.

I could see Michael Drake. He was either dead or unconscious in bed in the forward cabin. A small portable propane heater running at maximum output lay on its side on the floor nearby. The cabin was full of thick, acrid smoke from melted plastic and burned materials. The windows were all shut tight, and, as we learned later, the houseboat's ventilation system had been deliberately sabotaged—the intake vents were blocked with rags, and exhaust fans had been disconnected. The carbon monoxide detector on the wall was beeping weakly, its display showing dangerous levels of the deadly gas.

"Carbon monoxide poisoning," Kate said as paramedics wearing breathing gear carried the unconscious Drake out and laid him on the dock and began working to revive him. He was alive, but barely.

"Accident?" she asked some thirty minutes later. "Attempted murder or just a coincidence?"

"You know how I feel about coincidences," I replied. "No, given the timing and the extent of the sabotage, I'd say attempted murder," I said, watching as the paramedics administered oxygen to Drake and prepared him for transport to Erlanger Hospital. "Someone really didn't want us talking to him."

The fire department ventilated the houseboat while we waited. Samson stood quietly by, watching intently.

The paramedic's preliminary assessment of Drake's condition was severe carbon monoxide poisoning and smoke inhalation, but his vital signs were stable and the medical team was optimistic about his chances for recovery. Kate informed them he wasn't to be left alone and arranged for a guard to be stationed, round the clock, outside his hospital room door.

"Captain," Lt. Patterson, in charge of the fire department's first response team, called, "you need to see this."

We followed him into what appeared to be Drake's home office, a converted cabin that had been thoroughly ransacked. File cabinets had been forced open and emptied, papers scattered across the floor, and his computer equipment was conspicuously missing. Books had been pulled from shelves, desk drawers dumped out, and even the couch cushions had been slashed open.

"Looks like a professional search," I observed. "They were looking for something specific."

Kate nodded. "And it looks like they were in a hurry."

"Look over here," Patterson said, leading us to what appeared to be an empty corner of the office. "Look at this wall panel."

He pressed against what looked like a solid wood panel, and it slid sideways to reveal a hidden compartment containing a small fireproof safe, maybe two feet square.

"Looks like our environmental journalist was more paranoid than his attacker realized," I said.

Kate called for a locksmith to open the safe while I examined the rest of the houseboat with Patterson. The damage to the ventilation system was obviously deliberate. Someone with knowledge of boat systems had disabled the air circulator, blocked the air intakes, and then tipped over the electric heater.

"This was designed to look like an accident," Patterson

explained. "Old boat, illegal heater, blocked vents due to poor maintenance. Without a detailed investigation, it would have been ruled accidental death due to carbon monoxide poisoning."

"How long would it take to kill someone this way?" Kate asked.

"In an enclosed space this size, with the vents blocked and the heater running full blast? Maybe an hour, two at most. Drake was lucky. If you hadn't found him when you did, he'd be dead."

The locksmith arrived within the hour and successfully opened the fireproof safe to reveal a treasure trove of investigative materials. Dozens of files and photographs, computer storage devices, and what appeared to be audio recordings were neatly organized inside the compact safe.

"It looks to me like Drake wasn't just investigating environmental crimes," Kate said as she examined the file labels. "He was building legal cases. Look at these categories: 'Tennessee River Contamination,' 'Ashcroft Chemical Evidence,' 'Witness Statements,' 'Financial Records.'"

I picked up the thickest file, labeled "Tennessee River Contamination—Ashcroft Chemical Operations." It contained water quality reports spanning three years, photographs of dumping sites taken at night with telephoto lenses, and what appeared to be financial records showing payments to boat captains, waste disposal companies, and what were listed as "environmental consultants."

"Drake was building a federal case against Ashcroft Chemical," I said, scanning through documents that detailed systematic illegal dumping operations. "This represents years of investigation and documentation."

"And look at the timeline," Kate said, pointing to dates on

the reports. "The illegal dumping has been going on for decades, but it intensified dramatically after Victoria took over the company fifteen years ago."

One handwritten note particularly caught my attention. It was dated just five days earlier: "Meeting with Dr. J. Parker Saturday evening—8 PM at aquarium. She says she has definitive proof of systematic poisoning of river ecosystem. Chemical signatures match Ashcroft operations. EPA will have to act on this evidence."

"So Drake knew exactly what Dr. Parker had discovered," Kate said. "And he was planning to coordinate their evidence for a joint presentation to federal authorities."

"No wonder someone tried to kill him," I said. "Between Drake's investigation and Parker's scientific evidence, they had enough to bring down Ashcroft Chemical and probably send Victoria to prison."

My phone buzzed with a text message from TJ: *Someone's been watching your house. White sedan, different plates each day. Professional surveillance. Want me to check it out?*

I showed the message to Kate, then replied to TJ: *Don't approach. Document everything—license plates, occupants, timing, equipment. Stay safe and keep me posted.*

"We're definitely rattling some cages," Kate said, reading over my shoulder.

"Yeah, and whoever we're dealing with has serious resources and connections," I replied. "Professional surveillance, sophisticated security hacking, access to marine toxins, enough political influence to pressure the chief, and now attempted murder to silence witnesses."

We spent the rest of Tuesday afternoon carefully reviewing Drake's investigative files and cross-referencing them with Dr. Parker's research. The two investigations had covered much of the same ground, focusing on systematic chemical dumping in the remote creek systems west of Raccoon Mountain that fed into the Tennessee River.

The evidence was not just compelling, it was overwhelming. Someone had been using the isolated waterways as a private disposal system for industrial waste, coordinating dumping operations with Tennessee Valley Authority dam release schedules to ensure rapid dilution and dispersal of contaminants. The level of planning and technical knowledge required was impressive and disturbing.

"Look at these water flow calculations," I said, studying the maps that showed the dumping locations, current patterns, and timing charts coordinated with dam operations. "Whoever's behind this understands hydrology, chemistry, environmental science, and Tennessee Valley Authority operating procedures. This isn't some fly-by-night operation."

"And they've been doing it for decades," Kate added, reviewing financial records that showed regular payments to boat operators and disposal companies. "The amounts are staggering. We're talking about millions of dollars in illegal waste disposal fees over the years."

"Which explains why they're willing to kill to protect it," I said.

Tim called just before five o'clock with an update on his computer analysis of the aquarium's security system and his investigation into Ashcroft Chemical's digital infrastructure.

"The hacking was definitely professional-grade," he said, sounding excited. "It's military-grade encryption, sophisticated malware designed specifically for the aquarium's security system, and knowledge of vulnerabilities that aren't publicly available. This wasn't some kid with a laptop and a YouTube tutorial."

"Any idea who might have that kind of expertise?" Kate asked.

"Several possibilities, none of them good," Tim replied. "Could be corporate espionage specialists—there are companies that do this kind of work for hire. Could be former government cybersecurity people who've gone private. Could be someone with serious connections to organized crime. The techniques and tools suggest professional training and access to resources most hackers don't have."

"What about specific connections to Ashcroft Chemical?" I asked.

"That's where it gets really interesting," Tim said, and I could hear the sound of keyboard typing in the background. "Ashcroft Chemical's IT infrastructure is locked down tighter than a federal facility, but I've been finding some fascinating patterns in their business relationships. They contract with several companies that specialize in what they euphemistically call 'corporate security services' and 'risk management consulting.'"

"What kind of services?" Kate asked.

"The kind legitimate businesses don't usually need," Tim replied. "Background investigations that go way beyond normal employment screening. 'Reputation management' services that sound a lot like intimidation and harassment. 'Information security' consulting that could easily include surveillance and hacking. And payments to what appear to be shell companies with no obvious business purpose."

"Keep digging," Kate said. "But be careful. If they can hack the aquarium's system and attempt murder, they might be monitoring our communications too."

"Already thought of that," Tim said. "I'm routing everything through encrypted proxies and using techniques that would make the NSA proud. If they're monitoring us, they're going to have to work for it."

————

KATE CALLED me later that afternoon with an update from the hospital.

"Drake's condition has stabilized, but he's still unconscious," she said. "The doctors have him in a medically induced coma to help his brain recover from the carbon monoxide poisoning. They're optimistic, but he won't be able to answer questions for at least a week, maybe longer."

"So we're on our own for now," I said.

"Looks that way. But I've been going through more of his files from the safe, and they confirm our worst suspicions about the systematic dumping operation. Drake had documented everything - chemical signatures, timing patterns coordinated with dam releases, financial records showing payments to boat operators."

"Sounds the same as Dr. Parker," I said.

"Exactly. And the coordination between their two investigations suggests they were close to building an airtight federal case against whoever's behind this."

"Which explains why someone was desperate enough to kill Parker and try to kill Drake," I muttered thoughtfully.

"Drake's neurologist says when he does wake up, he might have memory issues from the carbon monoxide exposure," Kate continued. "So, we may never know exactly what he and Dr. Parker discussed about her research."

"But his files speak for themselves," I said. "Even if Drake can't remember specific conversations, we still have the evidence he collected."

"Maybe we'll get lucky and he'll wake up in pristine condition," she said. "Look, I need to go home and so do you. We'll talk in the morning, okay?"

I told her to have a good night and then hung up. Two minutes later my phone rang again. It was TJ.

"Harry, we've got a problem," he said. "The surveillance on your house has stepped up. There are two vehicles now, and they're not being subtle about it anymore. They're also watching Kate's place."

"Any idea who they're working for?" I asked.

"Not yet, but I've got photos and license plate numbers. Tim's running them through various databases. What I can tell you is that these aren't local private investigators or small-time operators. This is corporate-level surveillance with serious funding behind it."

"Stay safe, TJ. Don't take any unnecessary risks."

"You too, boss. These people have already tried to kill one journalist. They might decide that a private investigator and a police captain are worth the risk too."

It was almost seven that evening, and I was on my feet and ready to leave, when Lt. Patterson called. "Harry," he said. "Sorry to call so late, but I thought you'd like to know how I think it was done."

"Well, of course," I replied as I sat down again. "Thank you."

"There were two coffee mugs on the counter," he began. "One with dregs that tested positive for a strong sedative. It looks like Drake was entertaining his attacker who probably slipped the drug into his coffee, and then waited for him to pass out. Then they had all the time in the world to bring in the propane heater, sabotage the boat's safety systems and block the ventilation. Whether Drake knew his visitor or they talked their way in somehow, we can't tell yet. But whoever did this came prepared. They brought the heater and the sedative and they knew exactly how to disable the boat's systems."

"So this was definitely premeditated," I said.

"Oh yeah. This wasn't some spur-of-the-moment attack. Someone planned it carefully and executed it perfectly. If you hadn't found him when you did, Drake would be dead, and it would have looked like a tragic accident: an illegal heater and blocked vents. Bad boatmanship. Thing is, this kind of thing actually happens, so no one would have questioned it. "

As I sat in my office that evening, looking out at the Tennessee River flowing peacefully past downtown Chattanooga, and I realized, not for the first time, that we were facing something much more dangerous and complex than a simple murder case. Dr. Jennifer Parker had been killed because she'd discovered an environmental crime that threatened to expose decades of illegal dumping and corporate corruption. But her death had only been the beginning.

Now Michael Drake was lying in a hospital bed, in a coma, in a determined effort to silence him. Political pressure was being applied to limit our official inquiry. And professional surveillance teams were monitoring our movements and communications.

4

Downstream

Thursday/Friday

THURSDAY MORNING BEGAN WITH BETTER NEWS THAN I'D expected. Kate called at eight AM with an update from Erlanger Hospital.

"Drake's responding well to treatment," she said. "The doctors brought him out of the medically induced coma around six this morning. He's conscious and coherent, though still pretty weak."

"That's great news," I replied. Does he have any memory of what happened?"

"Not so much. He remembers having coffee with someone Tuesday evening, but the sedatives have affected his short-term memory. He can't recall who his visitor was or what they talked about. The doctors say his memory might come back gradually as he recovers."

"But he's talking?"

"Yes, he is. But he's weak, and he's scared as hell. He knows someone tried to kill him, even if he can't remember the details. He's agreed to have a police guard, and he wants to share everything he knows about the Ashcroft Chemical investigation."

I was relieved that Drake had survived the attempt on his life, but frustrated that his memory loss meant we'd lost crucial information about his attacker. Still, his investigative files had provided a wealth of evidence about the illegal dumping operation, and I was looking forward to his cooperation.

"Any word on Dr. Jones?" I asked.

We'd been trying to contact Dr. Wiley Jones since Tuesday to follow up on his nervous behavior at the crime scene, but he hadn't returned our calls.

"That's actually why I'm calling. I sent Corbin over to the aquarium this morning to track him down. Jones didn't show up for work yesterday or today, and his supervisor is getting worried."

"Maybe he's sick?" I said.

"Maybe. But Corbin went by his apartment, and the landlord says Jones moved out sometime Tuesday night or Wednesday morning. Packed up everything and left without giving notice. Lost his security deposit."

A chill ran down my spine. "He ran."

"It looks that way," she replied. "His apartment showed signs of hasty packing: clothes left behind, food still in the refrigerator, mail scattered on the floor. Corbin says it looked like he left in a hurry."

"Sounds like he was scared," I muttered.

"My thinking exactly," she replied. "The question is

whether Jones was running from us or from whoever killed Dr. Parker."

I thought about Jones' nervous behavior at the aquarium, his obvious discomfort when Victoria Ashcroft was around, and his knowledge of marine biology that would include familiarity with tetrodotoxin. He'd been on our suspect list, but his disappearance suggested something more complex.

"Kate," I said, "what if Jones wasn't the killer? If not, he could know something that makes him dangerous to the real killer?"

"You mean like Dr. Parker might have confided in him about her research?" she asked.

"Or maybe Jones discovered something on his own," I replied. "He worked at the aquarium. He had access to the same environmental data Parker was collecting. If he figured out who was behind the dumping operation..."

"He'd be another potential witness who needed to be silenced," Kate finished for me. "Just like Drake."

"Except Jones was smart enough to run before anyone could get to him," I said.

Kate was quiet for a moment, then said, "Corbin's going through Jones' office at the aquarium. Maybe he left something behind that will tell us what he's so afraid of."

"I'll meet you there. What time?"

"Give me an hour. I want to check on Drake first, see if his memory's improved at all."

An hour and a half later, Kate, Samson, and I were standing in Dr. Wiley Jones' small office at the Tennessee Aquarium. The space was cramped but organized, with research journals, water quality reports, and marine biology textbooks neatly arranged on shelves and in filing cabinets.

Corbin was methodically going through Jones' desk

drawers while Kate and I examined his computer and filing system. Corbin was Kate's partner, a man who treated crime scenes like archaeological digs and never missed important details.

"Interesting guy," Corbin said, holding up a photograph from Jones' desk. "Lives alone, no family pictures, but look at this."

The photograph showed Jones wearing a white coat and safety glasses standing next to what appeared to be a sophisticated laboratory setup. He was smiling broadly, holding up a test tube filled with clear liquid.

"That's not the aquarium's lab," Kate observed. "The equipment's too sophisticated, and I don't recognize the location."

I studied the photo more carefully. "Look at the background. Those tanks and that filtration system: it looks like a private research facility, not a public aquarium."

"Maybe Jones had a side job," Corbin suggested. "Or maybe he was doing research for someone else."

Kate's phone rang while we were examining Jones' files. She answered it on speaker.

"Captain Gazzara."

"Kate, it's Tim. I've got some information about Dr. Wiley Jones for you."

"What kind of information?"

"I've been digging into his background like you asked, and there are some red flags. Jones has been making regular deposits into his checking account over the past six months: cash deposits, always under the reporting threshold, but they add up to about thirty thousand dollars."

Kate and I looked at each other. "That's a lot of extra income for an aquarium researcher," I said.

"And there's more," Tim continued. "I traced his recent

activity, and Jones has been in contact with a shell company called Environmental Solutions LLC. They've been paying him as a consultant, supposedly for water quality analysis work."

"Let me guess," Kate said. "Environmental Solutions LLC is connected to Ashcroft Chemical."

"Bingo. It's one of several subsidiaries that Victoria Ashcroft uses for what she calls 'special projects.' The company has no physical address, no employees other than Jones, and no apparent business purpose other than paying him money."

I felt the pieces of the puzzle starting to shift into place. "So Jones was working for Victoria Ashcroft. He must have been her inside man at the aquarium."

"That would explain his nervous behavior," Kate said. "And why he ran when Dr. Parker was murdered."

"If Jones was feeding information to Victoria about the environmental research being conducted at the aquarium, he'd know exactly what Dr. Parker had discovered," I added. "He'd also know that he was now a liability to Victoria's operation."

Corbin looked up from Jones' computer. "That would explain something I found in his emails. Look at this."

He turned the computer screen toward us, showing an email dated last Friday, the day before Dr. Parker's murder. The message was from an address I didn't recognize, but the content was alarming.

"The Parker situation needs to be resolved immediately. She's gotten too close to information that could expose the entire opera-tion. We need to know exactly what she's planning and who she's been talking to. Your continued cooperation is essential."

"So Jones was spying on Dr. Parker for Victoria," Kate said

grimly. "He was reporting on her research, her plans, probably even her personal relationships."

"But if Jones was working for Victoria, why did he run?" Corbin asked.

"Because he realized he'd helped set up Dr. Parker's death," Kate replied. "And he knew that Victoria wouldn't hesitate to eliminate him too if he became inconvenient."

———

IT WAS THE FOLLOWING AFTERNOON, Friday, and I was in Kate's office when my phone buzzed with a text from TJ: "Found Jones. He's at Chickamauga Dam. You need to get here now."

I showed the message to Kate. "TJ found him."

"Is he alive?" Kate asked, already heading for the door.

"Let's find out."

Twenty minutes later, we were standing on the access road near Chickamauga Dam, looking down at the Tennessee River where it pooled behind the massive concrete structure. TJ was waiting for us next to his truck, his expression grim.

"He's down there," TJ said, pointing to a section of the riverbank several hundred yards downstream from the dam. "A fisherman spotted him around noon and called it in. Hamilton County Sheriff's department responded, but when they ran the name, it came back connected to your aquarium case."

Kate called for the medical examiner and crime scene team while Samson and I followed TJ down to the riverbank. The body was caught in fallen timber near the shore, partially submerged but clearly visible.

Dr. Wiley Jones was dead, his body showing the telltale signs of having been in the water for at least twenty-four hours. But even from a distance, I could see that this wasn't an accidental drowning.

"Looks like he was killed somewhere else and dumped here," TJ observed. "The current carried him downstream from wherever he went in."

Kate joined us at the water's edge, with Samson pacing restlessly beside her. "Same killer?" she asked.

"I'd bet on it," I replied. "Someone who knew Jones was a liability and decided to clean up loose ends."

Dr. Hensley arrived with the crime scene team some thirty minutes later. She worked steadily and methodically, documenting everything before she allowed the body to be moved.

"My preliminary examination suggests he died from respiratory failure," she said after her initial assessment. "I'll need to do a full autopsy to determine the exact cause, but I'm seeing signs that are consistent with the same tetrodotoxin poisoning that killed Dr. Parker."

"Same killer, same method," Kate said, thoughtfully.

"It's possible," Hensley replied. "I'll know more after I can examine him properly, but the external signs are similar: muscle rigidity, facial expression consistent with paralysis, no obvious trauma or defensive wounds."

"Time of death?" I asked.

"Hard to say precisely because of the water temperature and submersion, but probably sometime Tuesday night or early Wednesday morning. The body's been in the water at least twenty-four hours, possibly longer."

I nodded. That timeline fit with Jones' hasty departure from his apartment. He'd tried to run, but Victoria—or whoever was working for her—had caught up with him before he could get away.

"Any idea where he might have been killed?" Kate asked.

Dr. Hensley looked upstream toward the dam. "I'm thinking he must have gone into the water close to where we are now. Given the current patterns from the dam, I'd say that the backwash kept him close to the riverbank and he finally ended up in the debris where the fisherman found him."

TJ stood with his hands in his pants pockets, staring at the dam just a few hundred yards away. "Could have been anywhere this side of the river between here and the dam. You'll need to process this entire stretch of riverbank. "

Kate, standing beside TJ, nodded, heaved a sigh, and said, "Geez, I'm glad it's Mike and not me that has to do it. Still, maybe we'll get lucky and find some evidence."

As the paramedics set to work to recover Jones' body, I thought about the timeline of events. *Dr. Parker was murdered Saturday night after threatening to expose Victoria's illegal dumping operation. Someone tried to kill Drake on Tuesday evening to stop him from continuing his investigation. And now Jones— Victoria's inside man at the aquarium. Had he been killed simply to eliminate a loose end? Maybe!*

"Kate," I said, "I think this may be part of some sort of cleanup operation. Someone is eliminating anyone who could connect them to the environmental crimes or Dr. Parker's murder."

"If that's true, it means Drake is still in danger," she replied, "even with police protection."

"And so are we," I said. "If whoever killed Dr. Parker thinks we're getting too close to the truth, then it's only logical they'd come after us, too. We already know our homes are being watched. Maybe we should bring the watchers in."

"As long as they're just sitting there, we don't have probable cause, but you knew that, didn't you, Harry?"

I was about to respond with a smart remark when Kate's

radio crackled and a voice said, "Captain, this is Officer Martinez. I'm at Erlanger watching Mr. Drake... Look, Captain, I may be paranoid, but I think you should know that someone just tried to get into Drake's room. It was a woman who claimed to be a doctor—she was dressed like one, even had a stethoscope hung around her neck—but when I asked for her ID, she left. I've increased security, but I thought you should know."

She keyed the radio and said, "Well done, Martinez. Keep your eyes open and don't let anyone in you don't know."

"You got it, ma'am," Martinez came back.

Kate and I looked at each other grimly. "This is not good," she said.

"No, it's not," I replied. "And they're getting desperate, which makes them even more dangerous."

As we drove back into Chattanooga late that afternoon, Kate's phone rang with a call from Chief Johnston.

"Kate, I need to see you in my office first thing Monday morning," Johnston said without preamble. "And bring Harry with you."

The call ended abruptly, leaving Kate and me wondering what new political pressure was about to be applied to our investigation.

"I guess someone's been busy making phone calls," Kate said.

"Whoever's behind this has connections and influence. They're probably calling in every favor they can to shut us down."

"Well, they're about to find out that dead witnesses and attempted murders tend to make police chiefs less responsive to political pressure."

I hoped Kate was right, but I had a feeling that our next

meeting with Chief Johnston was going to be more challenging than our last one. Whoever was behind these murders clearly had the resources and connections to make life very difficult for anyone who threatened their operation.

As we pulled into the police department parking lot, I noticed TJ's truck following us. He'd been keeping watch over Kate and me, and his presence was reassuring given the escalating danger we were facing.

As we walked into the police department, I couldn't shake the feeling that we were just beginning to understand how dangerous and complex this case really was. Dr. Jones' murder had eliminated someone who clearly knew more than he should have about the environmental crimes. But it had also confirmed that we were dealing with killers who wouldn't hesitate to eliminate anyone who threatened them.

The question was whether Kate and I could stay ahead of them long enough to identify them before they decided that we, too, had become inconvenient witnesses who needed to be eliminated.

5

Undertow

Monday, Week 2

THE WEEKEND HAD BEEN A BLUR OF POLITICAL PHONE CALLS, crime scene processing, and growing pressure from city officials who seemed more concerned about Chattanooga's image than catching a killer. By the Monday morning of our second week on the case, I was beginning to understand that we were dealing with an adversary who had resources and connections that extended far beyond simple murder.

It was almost eight-thirty and I was on my way to my offices when Kate called me with some news that wasn't entirely surprising but was deeply troubling nonetheless.

"I just got out of an hour-long meeting with Chief Johnston," she said. "The political pressure over the weekend was intense. The mayor's office, three city council members, even a county commissioner called to express 'concerns' about the direction of our investigation."

"Let me guess," I said. "They want us to focus on finding Dr. Parker's killer without pursuing the environmental crimes angle."

"Worse than that. They want us to consider the possibility that Dr. Parker's death was an isolated incident, possibly connected to personal relationships or academic disputes rather than corporate conspiracy."

I felt my blood pressure rising. "What about Jones? What about Drake? Are those isolated incidents too?"

"According to the official line, Jones' death could have been accidental. Maybe he fell into the river while trying to flee from questioning. And Drake's carbon monoxide poisoning could have been a coincidence, just faulty equipment on an old houseboat."

"That's complete bullshit, Kate."

"I know that, and you know that" she replied. "But we're going to have to prove it with evidence that can't be dismissed or explained away. And he's not done yet, he wants to see us both, like now."

I sighed, shook my head, and said, "I'll be there as soon as I can."

I dropped in at the office, brought Jacque, my business partner and PA, up to speed, had a quick cup of of coffee while I checked my email, and an hour after Kate called, I was sitting in Chief Johnston's office while he delivered what amounted to a carefully worded warning about the political realities we were facing.

"The Mayor's office has received multiple calls expressing concern about the direction of this investigation," Johnston began, staring at me. "There are questions about whether we're pursuing appropriate leads or allowing the case to become unnecessarily complicated."

"Chief," Kate said carefully, "we've got three deaths connected to environmental crimes involving millions of dollars in illegal dumping. This isn't complicated. It's systematic murder to cover up a massive criminal operation."

"That's speculation, Captain. What we have are two *apparent* murders and one accidental drowning, all possibly connected to some kind of research project at the university."

I couldn't stay quiet. "Accidental drowning? Jones was poisoned with the same toxin that killed Dr. Parker, then dumped in the river to make it look accidental."

Johnston finally looked at me directly. "That's Dr. Hensley's preliminary assessment, Harry. The full autopsy might well reveal something different."

"What about Jones being paid thirty thousand dollars by a shell company connected to Ashcroft Chemical?" Kate asked. "What about the email telling him to gather intelligence on Dr. Parker?"

"Business consulting and private communications don't constitute evidence of murder," Johnston replied. "You're building a conspiracy theory based on circumstantial evidence and speculation."

Kate and I exchanged glances.

"Chief," Kate said, "are you ordering us to limit our investigation?"

Johnston stood up and walked to his window and looked out over the fire department next door. "Look, I've been doing this job long enough to know when someone with serious money and connections is applying pressure. This isn't just routine political interference. It's organized, coordinated, and it's coming from people who can end careers, mine as well as yours, Kate."

He turned back to face us. "The mayor made it very clear that this department's budget and my own position could be... reviewed... if we don't handle this case with appropriate discretion. And when the mayor starts talking about budget reviews, that's not a suggestion."

"And if the environmental crimes are central to understanding the murders?" I asked.

"Then prove it beyond a reasonable doubt," he said.

"So what are you telling us?" Kate asked, though I could see she already knew the answer.

"I'm telling you to be careful," Johnston said. "Whoever's behind this has enough influence to reach city council members, the mayor's office, and probably the county commission. They've got lawyers on retainer who specialize in making police investigations disappear. One procedural mistake, one accusation you can't prove in court, and they'll not only shut us down, they'll destroy this department's credibility for years to come."

He sat back down, his expression grave. "But I'm also telling you that if someone's committing murder in my city, I want them caught. I didn't become a cop to back down from killers just because they wear expensive suits and donate to political campaigns. Just make sure when you come for them, you build a case so solid that all their lawyers and political connections won't matter."

Johnston leaned forward. "And understand this: if this goes sideways, if you make a move without ironclad evidence, I won't be able to protect you. So you'd better be absolutely certain about what you're doing before you do it."

As we left Johnston's office, Kate shook her head grimly.

"Well, at least we know where we stand. The chief's trying to protect us, but his hands are tied."

"He's walking a tightrope," I replied. "Trying to let us do our job while keeping the department from being destroyed by whoever's pulling strings behind the scenes."

"The scary part is how organized this pressure campaign is," Kate said as we walked down the hallway. "City council, mayor's office, probably county commissioners—that takes serious coordination and influence."

"And serious money," I added. "Whoever's behind these murders isn't just some lone killer covering their tracks. They've got the resources to wage political warfare against an entire police department."

Kate paused at her office door. "Johnston's right about one thing, though; we'd better make damn sure we have an airtight case before we make our move. Because we're not going to get a second chance."

"Which means we need federal help," I said. "EPA, FBI, maybe even the Justice Department. Local politics won't matter as much if we can get federal agencies involved."

"Assuming they can't reach that high," Kate replied. "But you're right. We need allies with more firepower than the Chattanooga Police Department."

Monday morning also brought both new developments and complications. Kate had news from the crime scene team that had processed the area around Chickamauga Dam. They'd found where Jones went into the water. Apparently, there was a boat ramp off the riverwalk about a hundred and fifty yards downstream from the dam, and maybe the same upstream from where TJ found the body."

"Any tire tracks?" I asked.

"Yes, partials," she replied. "Willis is working on it. Apparently, there's mud washed up onto the concrete, and it looks like a vehicle, not a boat trailer, backed right up to the water's edge. But the tracks were partially washed out by weekend boat traffic, but he thinks he can at least determine the type of vehicle. Maybe get a tread pattern if we're lucky."

"What about the autopsy results?" I asked. "Anything new?"

She shugged. "Not anything we didn't already expect. Hensley finished the full autopsy over the weekend. Confirmed tetrodotoxin poisoning, same as Dr. Parker. Jones was injected behind the left ear, identical method and location. She estimates he died between eleven PM Tuesday and two AM Wednesday of last week."

I made notes as Kate spoke. The timeline confirmed that Jones had been killed shortly after fleeing his apartment, probably before he could get very far.

"So our killer caught up with him quickly," I said. "Either they knew where he was going, or they were monitoring his movements."

"Or Jones contacted his killer himself, thinking he could negotiate or explain his way out of trouble," Kate suggested.

"That's possible, I suppose," I replied. "If Jones realized he'd helped set up Parker's murder, he might have tried to make a deal to save his own life."

Kate's radio crackled with a call from dispatch. "Captain Gazzara, we've got a break-in at the UTC Environmental Sciences building. A security guard has found signs of forced entry and is requesting police response."

Kate and I looked at each other. "Dr. Parker's office," she said.

"Someone's looking for something they didn't find the first time," I agreed.

Twenty minutes later, we were standing in the hallway

outside Dr. Parker's office with Samson and a very nervous security guard named Pete Morrison. The door to the office had been forced open, but whoever had broken in had been more careful this time.

"It must have happened sometime Sunday evening," Morrison explained. "I do my regular rounds at eight, everything was normal. I come in Monday morning, find the door like this."

"Did you see anyone suspicious hanging around over the weekend?" Kate asked.

"No ma'am. The building's usually empty except for a few graduate students and faculty members who come in to check on research projects."

Kate turned Samson loose, and he trotted into Parker's office, nose twitching. Kate and I followed, to find it had been thoroughly searched since our last visit. File cabinets had been emptied, desk drawers pulled out, and even the ceiling tiles had been moved. But unlike the ransacked houseboat, this search had been methodical and professional.

"They took their time," I observed.

"The question is, did they find what they were looking for?" Kate said, examining the empty filing cabinets.

Samson was pacing restlessly around the office, picking up scents and traces that weren't apparent to us. "Look at that," I said to Kate, I'd say it was more than one person did this."

She nodded but didn't reply. She was frowning deeply, her eyes narrowed, her lips pinched together. Lovely as she is, it wasn't a pretty look.

"Kate," I said, studying the pattern of the search, "what if we're looking at this the wrong way? What if they weren't looking for her evidence? What if someone was looking for research data or files that could be used to continue her work?"

"You mean like someone who wanted to pick up where she left off?" Kate asked, her brow still furrowed.

"Exactly! Or maybe it was someone who wanted to make sure no one else could continue her investigation."

"Geez, Harry," she said with an exasperated look on her face. "You're not making it any easier."

I grinned at her. "Nothing about what we do is ever easy; you know that."

My phone buzzed with a call from Tim.

"Tim. What's up?"

"Harry, I've got some interesting news about that shell company, Environmental Solutions LLC."

"Go on," I said.

"It's crazy," he said. "The company was dissolved last Friday, three days after Dr. Parker's murder. All the assets were transferred to another shell company, all the records were sealed, and all financial connections were severed."

Kate had moved closer to listen. "They're covering their tracks," she said.

"I found similar patterns with two other companies connected to Ashcroft Chemical," he continued. "Both were dissolved within days of Dr. Parker's death, both had been making payments to individuals who might have had access to environmental research data."

"How many people are we talking about?" I asked.

"At least a dozen over the past three years," he replied. "Payments ranging from a few thousand to over fifty thousand dollars. All for consulting work, all paid through shell companies with no obvious business purpose."

I frowned as I considered the implications of what Tim

had revealed. "Tim, d'you have any idea what Victoria Ashcroft was doing? Was she buying information from researchers and scientists? Or was she maybe buying security?"

"Your guess is as good as mine, Harry," he replied.

"I think she was building an intelligence network," Kate said. "It could be she was having anyone working on environmental issues that might threaten Ashcroft Chemical's operations watched."

"That's a hell of a stretch, Kate," I said, "but it's worth considering."

After hanging up with Tim, Kate and I continued examining Dr. Parker's office. The thoroughness of the search suggested that whoever had broken in had considerable knowledge of academic research practices and knew exactly what kinds of files and data to look for.

"Harry," Kate said from behind Parker's desk, "look at this."

She was holding a small piece of paper that had apparently fallen behind one of the desk drawers. It appeared to be a note written in Parker's hand:

S.H. - Environmental data backup stored at off-site location. Access code: Neptune2024. Use only if primary files compromised.

"S.H.," I said. "Sally Howard."

"I'm thinking Parker was giving her girlfriend access to backup copies of her research," Kate said. "Smart, considering what happened to her primary files."

"We should talk to Dr. Howard again," I said. "If she has Parker's backup research data, she might have information that could help us understand exactly what Parker discovered."

As we prepared to leave the Environmental Sciences building, I noticed a woman in a dark coat watching us from across the parking lot. She was too far away to make out clearly, but something about her posture and the way she quickly looked away when she saw I'd noticed her seemed familiar.

"Kate," I said, nodding toward the parking lot, "we've got an observer."

By the time Kate looked in that direction, the woman had gotten into a small sedan and was driving away. The distance and angle made it impossible to get the license plate number, but I noted it was a dark-colored compact car, probably a Honda or Toyota.

"Someone's keeping tabs on us," Kate said.

"Or someone's very interested in what we might find in Dr. Parker's office."

We drove to the marine biology building to interview Dr. Sally Howard about the backup research data. The building was quiet. It was after all Monday afternoon, and it was populated with only a few students and faculty members walking this way and that along the hallways.

Dr. Howard's office was on the third floor, a small space with the walls lined with shelves and file cabinets filled with marine biology textbooks, research journals, and photographs of underwater ecosystems. She was grading papers when we knocked, and she looked genuinely surprised to see us.

"Captain Gazzara, Mr. Starke," she said, gesturing for us to sit down. "I wasn't expecting to see you again so soon. Is there news about what happened to Jennifer?"

"It's early days yet," Kate replied, "but we're following up on some new information," Kate said. She paused for a moment, then continued, "Dr. Howard, we found a note in Dr. Parker's office. She gave you backup copies of her research data, didn't she?"

Sally's expression and demeanor became guarded. She frowned, then said, "Jennifer was very careful about her work. She knew that her environmental research could be controversial, especially when it involved large, local corporations."

"So did she give you access to backup files?" I asked.

Sally hesitated again, then nodded. "She asked me to keep copies of her most important research, just in case something happened to her primary files. She said she was worried about industrial espionage or corporate interference."

"Industrial espionage," Kate repeated. "Did she mention any specific companies or individuals she was concerned about?"

"Mostly Ashcroft Chemical and their subsidiaries. Jennifer had become convinced that they were not just dumping illegally, but actively trying to suppress research that could expose their operations."

"Can you explain that?" I asked.

"She was sure Victoria Ashcroft was buying information from so-called researchers, pressuring university administrators to limit environmental studies, even hiring private investigators to monitor scientists who were getting too close to sensitive information."

I thought about Dr. Jones and the payments he'd been receiving from Environmental Solutions LLC. "Did Dr. Parker know about other researchers who might have been compromised?"

Sally's expression darkened further. "She suspected several people, but she didn't have proof. She said the only way to stay safe was to keep her most important findings secret until she could present them to federal authorities."

"Dr. Howard," Kate said, "we need copies of those backup

files. They might contain evidence that could help us identify Dr. Parker's killer. They're in digital format, I presume."

"I understand," she replied, "but Jennifer made me promise to only release the data to EPA investigators or federal prosecutors. She was very specific about that."

"Dr. Parker is dead, Sally," I said gently. "And whoever killed her is systematically eliminating anyone who might have access to her research. You could be in danger if the killer thinks you have information that could threaten their operation."

She was quiet for a long moment, clearly wrestling with competing loyalties. "The files are stored at a secure off-site location. I can access them, but I'd want some kind of official assurance that they'll be used appropriately."

"We can arrange for federal authorities to review the material," Kate said. "But we need to act quickly. Dr. Jones is dead. We think he was murdered because he had information about Dr. Parker's research. You might be the next target."

"Dr. Jones is dead?" Sally repeated, her voice barely above a whisper.

"Murdered with the same poison that killed Dr. Parker," Kate confirmed. "We found evidence that he'd been feeding information to Ashcroft Chemical about environmental research at the aquarium."

Sally's composure cracked slightly, and I could see fear in her eyes. "Jennifer was right. They really are killing anyone who threatens them. I thought she was being paranoid, but now..."

"Which is why we need your help," I said. "The backup research data might be the key to exposing whoever's behind these murders."

Sally finally agreed to retrieve the backup files and make

copies available to us and federal investigators, but she insisted on additional security measures. Kate arranged for unmarked patrol units to monitor Sally's apartment and office, and I asked TJ to add Dr. Howard to his informal surveillance rotation.

A few moments later, as we were about to leave the marine biology building, Kate received a call from Dr. Hensley.

"Dr. Hensley," Kate said. "What can I do for you?"

"I found something I thought you should know about," Hensley said. "Jones had defensive wounds on his hands and arms; he fought with his attacker before being injected with the tetrodotoxin."

"So he knew his killer was going to harm him," Kate muttered thoughtfully.

"I think so," she replied. "There was also skin and blood under his fingernails. If we can find a suspect, we should be able to make a match. Oh, and there's one more thing; we found a small encrypted thumb drive sewn into the lining of his jacket. Whoever killed him missed it during their search. I've sent it over to your computer specialist, Tim Clarke. Look, I have to go. I'll keep you informed." And he hung up.

"Some good news at last," I said.

"You hope," Kate said, cynically.

As we pulled into the police department parking lot, Kate's radio crackled with an urgent message from Officer Martinez.

"Captain, we've got a situation at Erlanger Hospital. Someone attempted to gain access to Michael Drake's room again. I think you'd better come. Hospital security is having a hissy."

Kate and I looked at each other grimly. "They're not giving up on Drake, are they?" she said.

"Either that or they didn't find what they were looking for on the boat and they're getting desperate enough to take bigger risks," I replied.

As we raced toward the hospital with lights flashing and sirens blaring, I couldn't shake the feeling that we were always one step behind a killer who seemed to anticipate our every move. The question was whether we could identify and stop them before the body count rose any higher.

6

Storm Warnings

Wednesday

WEDNESDAY MORNING BROUGHT A BREAKTHROUGH THAT BOTH vindicated our investigation and raised the stakes considerably. It was seven-thirty and I was in my home office when Tim called me, his voice bubbling with excitement.

"Harry," he squeaked, "I've cracked Jones' encrypted files from that thumb drive Dr. Hensley sent over. You're not going to believe what this guy documented."

"Give me the highlights," I replied, already reaching for my jacket.

"Systematic chemical waste dumping coordinated with Tennessee Valley Authority dam release schedules going back three years. Jones kept meticulous records—dates, times, chemical signatures, even photographs taken of the boats involved with a telephoto lens. "

I felt my pulse quicken. "Boats?" I asked. "What boats? I need names."

"No names, Harry, just boats conducting dumping operations at night. But get this: one of the boat captains is clearly identifiable in several shots. I was able to identify him as Frank Muldoon. He operates out of Chickamauga Marina. The same marina where Drake keeps his houseboat."

"Any connection to Ashcroft Chemical?" I asked.

"Oh yeah," he replied. "Jones documented payments from Environmental Solutions LLC—that shell company we tracked—totaling sixty-five thousand dollars over eighteen months. Muldoon was getting paid fifteen hundred per dumping operation. So was a guy with the last name Marsh; no first name mentioned."

Kate arrived at my office twenty minutes later with Samson, looking grim. "I just got off the phone with the EPA regional office in Atlanta," she said. "They're sending a team up here this afternoon to review the environmental evidence."

"That's good news, isn't it?"

"Maybe. The agent I spoke with, Rebecca Mornay, said they've had Ashcroft Chemical on their radar for years but never had enough evidence to build a case."

"Speaking of evidence," I said, "Tim called me earlier this morning. He's cracked the encrypted data from that thumb drive they found on Jones' body. He says Jones documented everything; dumping operations, financial records, even photographs of the boats, and payments to boat captains by the names of Marsh and Muldoon."

"Oh, that's fantastic," she replied. "If Dr. Jones' documentation is as complete as that, we might finally have them."

"And the EPA?" I said.

"I talked to Agent Mornay yesterday afternoon after Sally

Howard came through with Dr. Parker's backup research files. I transmitted everything to the EPA Tuesday evening. Mornay said Parker's data was exactly what they needed, but might not be enough, which is why she'll be here late this afternoon. But if Jones' files corroborate the dumping operations and provide additional evidence..." she trailed off, thinking. "You know... I don't want the EPA taking over my investigation. Maybe we should hold Jones' files back for a while."

"You know there's going to be political pressure, right?" I asked.

Kate's expression darkened. "Oh yeah. Chief Johnston got another round of calls last night. This time from the county commission chairman and two state legislators. Someone's really working the phones."

"Meaning we need to move fast before they shut us down completely," I said.

"Exactly," she replied.

Tim had made copies of Jones' most damning evidence and sent them to my computer. He'd also made a thumb drive for Kate. Jones' documentation was indeed meticulous. Apparently he'd been conducting his own private investigation even while feeding information to Victoria Ashcroft. Whether it was guilt, fear, or simple self-preservation, we'd never know.

"I mean, look at these thermal imaging shots," Tim said, spreading photographs across the conference table after pushing his glasses further up the bridge of his nose. "Jones somehow got access to satellite data that shows exactly where the dumping has been occurring. The chemical signatures match the contamination patterns Dr. Parker identified in her research."

I studied the images. "How did an aquarium marine biologist get access to satellite thermal imaging?"

"That's the interesting part," Tim replied. "As a marine biologist he had contacts at NOAA—the National Oceanic and Atmospheric Administration. He was using his legitimate research credentials to access the data."

"Maybe Jones was trying to build a dead man's switch to use against the people who were paying him, if it got out of hand," Kate suggested

Tim shrugged, did the thing with his glasses again, and said, "Either way, he did a good job of it," Tim continued. "The chemical composition of the waste materials, GPS coordinates of the dumping sites, even recordings of phone conversations with someone he identifies only as 'the boat captain.'"

"Frank Muldoon," I said.

"Has to be," Tim agreed, "or Marsh. And according to this timeline, the most recent dumping operation was scheduled for last Tuesday night; the same night Jones was murdered."

Kate and I exchanged glances. "Someone wanted to make sure Jones couldn't interfere with their operation," she said.

"Or couldn't testify against them," I added.

My phone buzzed with a text from TJ: "I found Muldoon. He's at the marina working on his boat. Want me to keep eyes on him?"

I showed the message to Kate. "We should talk to Muldoon before the EPA gets here," she said. "If he's been conducting the dumping operations, he might be willing to cooperate in exchange for immunity."

"Assuming he's still alive when they get there," I replied. "If whoever killed Jones and Parker is cleaning house, Muldoon is sure to be on their list."

"All the more reason to get to him quickly," she replied. "Come on. Let's get out of here."

"Keep digging, Tim," I said as I grabbed my jacket. "I'll be in later." *I hope,* I couldn't help but think.

I told Jacque goodbye and we left, leaving her open mouthed.

———

WE DROVE to Chickamauga Marina through a gray October morning that felt heavy with approaching storm clouds. The Tennessee River looked dark and restless under the overcast sky, and I couldn't help but think about all the toxic waste that had been dumped into these waters over the years.

The marina was busier than it had been during our previous visit to Drake's boat, with several boat owners preparing their vessels for winter storage or taking advantage of the cooler weather for fishing.

TJ was waiting for us in the marina parking lot, leaning against his truck with a pair of binoculars around his neck. He looked tired, like he'd been there for hours.

"Muldoon hasn't left since I got here an hour ago," he said. "He's been working on his boat, a thirty-eight foot cabin cruiser in slip forty-seven. It looks like he's getting it ready for something. He's loading supplies, checking equipment, fueling up. He's also been making phone calls, lots of them. And he keeps checking his watch like he's on some kind of schedule."

"Any idea who he's calling?" Kate asked.

"Too far away to hear, but his body language suggests he's not happy about whatever's being discussed. Lot of pacing, hand gestures, the kind of stuff you see when someone's arguing or getting pressured."

"Any sign there's anyone watching him?" Kate asked.

"Not that I can see," he replied, "but someone could be watching from the other side of the marina or from the water. This place has too many sight lines to cover alone." TJ paused, then added, "There is one thing, though. About an hour ago, a woman in a dark sedan drove through the marina parking lot real slow, like she was looking for someone. Same type of car you mentioned seeing at the university."

That caught my attention. "Did you get a look at her?"

"Not clearly. Tinted windows, and she kept her distance. But she circled the parking lot twice before driving off. Could be coincidence, but..."

"But you don't believe in coincidences any more than I do," I finished.

"Exactly."

"And you didn't get the license number?" I asked.

"Nope, couldn't do it without exposing myself."

I looked at Kate. She nodded.

"Come with us, TJ," I said, "but keep out of sight. We're expecting visitors, and they won't be friendly."

He pulled his jacket open to reveal his holstered CZ-75, let it fall back, then said, "How about you?"

I gave him a sly smile, showed him my CZ Shadow, and said, "Always! Watch your back."

We walked down the dock toward slip forty-seven, Samson trotting beside Kate. The marina was alive with the sound of boat engines, the smell of gasoline and marine oil, and the gentle lapping of water against hulls and dock pilings.

Frank Muldoon was exactly what I'd expected from the photographs in Jones' files: a weathered man in his fifties with the kind of deep tan that comes only from spending most of your life outdoors. His hands were stained and callused from years of working with ropes and equipment. He was wearing faded jeans, work boots, and a flannel shirt that had seen better days. When he saw us approaching, he was loading what appeared to be water testing equipment into the cabin of his boat, but I also spotted several heavy-duty plastic containers that looked out of place for normal research work.

"Frank Muldoon?" Kate asked, showing her badge.

Muldoon's eyes went immediately to Kate's badge, then to Samson, then to me. His expression shifted from casual curiosity to wariness in about three seconds, and I could see him calculating, trying to figure out how much trouble he might be in.

"Depends who's asking," he said.

"Captain Gazzara, Chattanooga Police," Kate replied. "We'd like to ask you some questions about your boat operations and your relationship with Dr. Wiley Jones."

Muldoon set down the equipment he'd been loading and wiped his hands on a greasy towel. The towel was already stained with what looked like chemical residue, not just engine oil. "I heard about Wiley. Terrible thing, him drowning like that. He was a good customer."

"Customer for what?" I asked, studying the various containers and equipment on his boat.

"Environmental consulting. I do water quality sampling for researchers, take them to sites that are hard to reach by land. Wiley hired me maybe once a month for the past couple years." He paused, then added defensively, "It's all legitimate work. I keep detailed logs, proper permits, an' all that."

Kate stepped closer. "Mr. Muldoon, we have evidence that Dr. Jones was documenting illegal chemical dumping operations in the Tennessee River system. Operations that involved your boat."

Muldoon's facade cracked slightly, and I could almost see the wheels spinning inside his head, calculating his odds, trying to decide how much we knew and what his best play might be.

"I don't know anything about illegal dumping," he said. "I provide legitimate boat services to researchers and environmental consultants."

"We have photographs," I said. "Taken with telephoto lenses. Your boat, your face, clearly identifiable."

"And we have financial records showing payments from shell companies connected to Ashcroft Chemical," Kate added.

Muldoon was quiet for a long moment, his hands working nervously with the towel. Finally, he looked around the marina as if checking for listeners, then nodded toward his boat.

"You better come aboard," he said quietly. "This isn't a conversation for the docks."

The cabin of Muldoon's boat was cramped but efficiently organized, with navigation equipment, marine radios, and what appeared to be sophisticated water monitoring gear mounted on custom brackets. The space smelled of diesel fuel, cleaning solvents, and something chemical that I couldn't identify. Charts of the Tennessee River system covered one wall, marked with numerous annotations in different colored ink. Some of the notations looked like standard navigation markers, but others appeared to be depth readings and current measurements in areas that wouldn't normally require such detailed documentation.

He gestured for us to sit at a small table while he remained standing, positioned where he could see through the cabin windows. His nervousness was becoming more apparent with sweat beading on his forehead despite the cool morning air, and hands that wouldn't stay still.

"Look," he said, his voice barely above a whisper, "I'm not a bad guy. I got two kids in college and a wife with medical bills that'll bankrupt us if I don't keep working. When someone offers you good money for boat work, you don't ask too many questions. You can't afford to."

"What kind of boat work?" Kate asked, her tone careful but insistent.

"Transportation. I was told it was treated wastewater being discharged in approved locations. I had paperwork that looked legitimate. You know? EPA permits, discharge authorizations, all properly signed and sealed. Hell, I even kept copies." He gestured toward a small filing cabinet mounted against one wall. "Everything looked official."

"Fake paperwork," I said.

"I didn't know that at the time," he replied, his voice rising slightly. "Hell, I don't know now. All I knew was that I was being paid fifteen hundred dollars a trip to transport materials from a treatment facility to designated discharge points. The money was good, the paperwork looked real, and I needed the work."

"How many trips?" Kate asked.

Muldoon hesitated, then said, "Maybe forty, fifty over the past three years. Usually at night, always coordinated with dam release schedules."

"Who hired you?"

"A woman who said she represented Environmental Solutions LLC. Professional type, well-dressed, drove an expensive car. She said they were conducting a pilot program for efficient wastewater disposal."

Kate and I exchanged glances. "Can you describe this woman?"

"Mid-fifties, silver hair, always wore business suits. Real confident, like she was used to being in charge. She handled all the payments and scheduling."

Victoria Ashcroft. It had to be. *Surely she couldn't have been doing it personally,* I thought. It was insane.

"Mr. Muldoon," Kate said, "the materials you were transporting weren't treated wastewater. They were industrial chemicals and toxic waste being dumped illegally into the Tennessee River."

Muldoon's face went pale. "Holy shit! You're frickin' serious?"

"Dead serious. And the man who was documenting these operations, Dr. Jones, was murdered Tuesday night."

"Murdered?" Muldoon's voice cracked. "Wiley was murdered? I thought he fell in off the fishing pier and drowned."

"No. He was killed with an injection of the same neurotoxin that killed Dr. Jennifer Parker," I said. "We think someone's eliminating anyone who can connect them to the illegal dumping."

Muldoon gulped, and sat down heavily in a chair across from us, his hands shaking slightly. "Oh God. Oh geez. What the hell have I gotten myself into?"

"The question is whether you're willing to help us expose whoever's behind the dumping," Kate said. "We can protect you, and if you cooperate fully, the prosecutor might be willing to work out a deal."

"Protection?" Muldoon laughed bitterly. "Lady, if these people killed Wiley Jones and Jen Parker, what makes you think they won't kill me too?"

"Because we'll keep you safe," I said. "But we need your cooperation and testimony to build a case that will stick."

Muldoon was quiet for several minutes, staring at his hands. Finally, he looked up at us with resignation in his eyes.

"What do you need to know?"

For the next hour, Kate recorded Muldoon as he provided details that corroborated and expanded on Jones' documentation. The dumping operation was sophisticated and extensive, involving multiple types of industrial waste, carefully planned routes, and coordination with TVA dam operations to ensure maximum dispersal of contaminants.

"The discharge points were always in remote areas," he said. "Creek systems that feed into the main river, places where the current would carry everything downstream quickly. Whoever planned this knew the river system inside and out."

"What about the materials themselves?" Kate asked. "Did you ever see what was actually being dumped?"

"Sealed containers, usually fifty-gallon drums or smaller chemical tanks. I was told never to open them or handle them directly. Everything was loaded and unloaded—I mean emptied—by workers at the treatment facility."

"Which treatment facility?" I asked.

"The Old Ashcroft Chemical plant west of Raccoon Mountain. It's been decommissioned for years, but they still use it for storage and equipment maintenance."

I made notes as Muldoon spoke. The decommissioned plant would explain how the operation could continue without detection: no regular employees, no routine inspections, no oversight from regulatory agencies.

"And you say you don't know who the woman who's been paying you is?" I asked.

"I've no idea," he replied.

I sighed, looked at Kate, then said, "When's your next scheduled run, Mr. Muldoon?"

"Tomorrow night. But I'm not doing it. Not after what you've told me, I'm done with this whole thing."

"Actually," Kate said, "you are. We need you to keep that appointment. With EPA oversight and police surveillance, so we can document the operation and gather evidence that will be admissible in court."

"You want me to risk my life to help you set up a sting operation?" he asked, obviously unable to believe what he was hearing.

"We want you to help us stop a criminal enterprise that's been poisoning the Tennessee River for years," Kate replied. "And we want to catch the people who murdered Dr. Parker and Dr. Jones before they kill anyone else."

Muldoon finally agreed to cooperate, though his reluctance was obvious. Kate arranged for protective surveillance and scheduled a meeting with the EPA team for later that afternoon.

As we prepared to leave Muldoon's boat, my phone rang with a call from Amanda.

"Harry, someone tried to break into our security system last night," she said, her voice tense. "Our home security company called me this morning. They said it was a professional job, very sophisticated. They got through the first two layers of security before the system locked them out and triggered the alarms."

I felt a chill run down my spine. "Are you and Jade safe?"

"We're fine. Maria's here, and we've increased security. The company's sending a tech out to upgrade the system, and I've called in some additional private security. But Harry, whoever's behind this is definitely escalating. They know where we live and they know our routines."

"Pack a bag for you and Jade," I said. "Go stay with August and Rose until this is over. "

"Harry—"

"Amanda, please," I snapped, interrupting her. "These people have already killed twice. I'm not taking any chances with you and Jade. And make sure you take Maria with you. They might target her too, just to get to us."

"All right," she said after a pause. "But I'm not running scared forever. We need to end this, and quickly."

"We will. I promise."

After I hung up, Kate looked at me with concern. "They're targeting your family now?"

"Looks that way," I replied. "Which means we're getting close to something they're desperate to protect."

"Or they're running out of time and getting sloppy," she replied, caustically.

As we walked back toward the marina parking lot, TJ approached us with a troubled expression.

"We've got a problem," he said. "I've been monitoring radio chatter, and there's been unusual activity around the old Ashcroft Chemical plant west of the dam. A lot more chatter than you'd expect for a decommissioned facility."

I thought about the implications. "Maybe they're planning to shut down the operation and eliminate the evidence."

My phone buzzed with a text from Tim: "Harry, when you get a chance, stop by the office. I've got some interesting details from Jones' files that might be helpful."

Kate read the message over my shoulder. "What now?" she asked.

"Probably just more documentation to add to what we

already know. Tim's been working through Jones' data non-stop."

TJ looked between us. "You want me to maintain surveillance on Muldoon, Harry?"

"Yes. Absolutely, but keep your distance," Kate said. "He knows way too much, and, if they're cleaning house, he could be next on the list. We might be the only thing keeping him alive right now. I'll call in and arrange protection for him."

As we drove back toward downtown Chattanooga, storm clouds continued to gather, and I had a feeling we were running out of time. Whoever was behind these murders was moving to protect themselves, and we still didn't have enough evidence to make arrests that would stick.

But we were getting closer. And with EPA backing, Muldoon's cooperation, and Tim's technical expertise, we might finally be able to build a case strong enough to overcome the political pressure and bring the killers to justice.

The question was whether we could do it before they decided that Kate and I had become too dangerous to leave alive.

Thunder rumbled in the distance as we pulled into the police department parking lot, and I couldn't help but think it sounded like a warning.

7

Breaking the Surface

Thursday

THURSDAY MORNING FOUND ME AT AUGUST'S HOME AT THE breakfast table with Amanda and Jade, trying to maintain some semblance of normal family life despite the escalating complexity of our investigation. August was out of town and Rose was in the kitchen. Maria was expected momentarily. Jade was picking at her scrambled eggs while Amanda was drinking coffee and scanning news reports on her tablet.

"Any developments overnight?" she asked, not looking up from her screen.

"Nothing yet," I replied, buttering Jade's toast. "But Kate and I are meeting with federal agents this morning. FBI, EPA, and I f…" I looked at Jade and then said, "I hate that."

"Federal agents?" Amanda looked up. "Harry, this case is escalating beyond anything I expected."

"Daddy, what's federal agents?" Jade interrupted, her green eyes wide with curiosity.

"Just some people who help solve big problems that cross state lines, sweetheart," I said, exchanging a glance with Amanda. "Like when bad guys do bad things in different places."

"Are you gonna catch the bad guys?"

"That's the plan, princess." I ruffled her hair. "The good guys always win, remember?"

Amanda waited until Jade was distracted with her breakfast before leaning closer. "Harry, if federal agencies are getting involved, this isn't just a local murder case anymore."

"I know that," I all but snapped, but then calmed down and said, "The environmental crimes are bigger than we initially realized."

"Just... be careful, okay? These people have already killed twice, and now they've tried to hack our security system."

The domestic tranquility was shattered when my phone rang. I glanced at the screen and saw TJ's number.

"TJ," I said, answering the call. "What's up?"

"Harry, we've got a serious problem," he said, his voice tight with urgency. "I've been watching Muldoon's boat all night like you asked, and around four this morning I saw someone tampering with it."

"No sh.." Again I paused and glanced at Jade before continuing. "Tampering how?"

"Someone was underneath the hull for about twenty minutes. I couldn't get close enough to see what they were doing without blowing my cover, but when they left, I went in for a look."

"And?"

"An explosive device," he replied. "Hidden in a locker

under the capstan, against the hull. It's small. Remote detonated. I've called the bomb squad, but, Harry, if Muldoon had taken that thing out on the water..."

I was already reaching for my jacket. "I'll be there in thirty minutes. And TJ?"

"Yeah?"

"Call—"

"Hold on, Harry" he said, interrupting me. "Ah... they're almost here. I can hear the sirens."

"Good. Now call Kate and ask her to meet us at the marina."

Amanda was staring at me with concern. "Explosives?" she whispered.

"I have to go," I said, kissing her and Jade goodbye. "Stay alert today, okay? And keep Maria close."

"Harry—"

"I'll call you later," I said, already heading for the door.

I hadn't been in the car five minutes when Kate called.

"I take it you heard from TJ?" I said.

"I did," she said, "but it gets worse. After TJ called the bomb squad, he found Muldoon's truck had been sabotaged too. Brake lines cut, steering fluid drained. Someone wanted to make sure he didn't survive the night, whether he tried to run or tried to cooperate with us."

A short while later, I was standing on the dock at Chickamauga Marina watching the bomb squad technicians carefully remove an explosive device from Frank Muldoon's boat. The marina had been evacuated as a precaution, and Kate had arranged for Muldoon to be moved to a safe house until we could figure out who wanted him dead.

"It's crude," Sergeant Williams from the bomb squad said, examining the device, "but it would have done the job. Gelignite, remote detonator with about a two-mile range." He shook his head. "I never would have believed it," he said.

Kate and I exchanged glances. "Victoria Ashcroft's security contractors," she said.

"Which means Victoria has access to explosives and professional operatives," I replied. "Geez, how much worse can it get?"

"Nah," Williams said. "This was cobbled together, not something a pro would do. They probably found the plans for it on the internet."

TJ approached us, looking tired but alert. He'd been watching Muldoon's boat for almost eighteen hours straight, and his vigilance had probably saved the boat captain's life.

"Harry, there's something else you need to know," he said. "The person who planted the bomb? I got a partial look at them through night vision. Average height, hoodie. Could be anyone with basic knowledge."

"Well, it wasn't Victoria, then," Kate said. "She's almost as tall as I am."

At that, I smiled. "She wouldn't do her own dirty work," I said. "She'd pay someone to do it for her." I looked at Williams and said, "Can I see that thing?"

He handed it to me. It only took a quick look to see he was right. Two sticks of gelignite, an old smart phone and a detonator all held together by four hefty rubber bands.

"Gelly," I said. "Used mainly for blasting in rock quarries. Powerful stuff." I handed the home-made bomb back to Williams. "And there are plenty of those around here," I finished.

"Quick and simple," he said.

I thought about the pattern of evidence we'd been seeing. "So we have some amateur making bombs, but we also have sophisticated surveillance and hacking operations. Either we're dealing with someone with mixed skills, or there are multiple people involved."

"That's what's bothering me," Kate said. "The inconsistency. Professional hacking and surveillance, but homemade explosives."

"And enough political influence to pressure city council members and the mayor's office," Kate added.

My phone buzzed with a call from Tim. "Harry, I've been digging deeper into Ashcroft Chemical's business relationships, and I found something concerning."

"What kind of concerning?"

"Victoria Ashcroft has been paying a private security contractor called Meridian Security Solutions for what they call 'comprehensive risk management.' We're talking about substantial monthly payments over the past two years."

Kate moved closer so she could hear. "What kind of risk management?" she asked.

"Corporate security, background investigations, threat assessment. But according to their website, they also provide 'discrete problem resolution for high-value clients.'"

"That's a euphemistic way of saying they handle problems that regular security companies won't touch," I said. "It means they do wetwork."

"Yeah, that," Tim agreed. "And you're probably right, because Meridian Solutions employs a lot of former military and intelligence personnel. People with exactly the kind of training you'd need for sophisticated surveillance operations."

Kate's radio crackled with an urgent message from dispatch. "Captain Gazzara, we're receiving reports of a boat in distress near the old Ashcroft Chemical plant. Wildlife is responding, but they're requesting police backup."

Kate and I looked at each other. "Too much of a coincidence," she said.

"You're right about that," I said.

We left the bomb squad to finish processing the explosive device and raced toward the river access road near the old Ashcroft Chemical plant. The facility sat on a bluff overlooking the Tennessee River, about five miles west of Chickamauga Dam. According to Muldoon's testimony, it had served as the staging area for the illegal dumping operations.

Two Tennessee Wildlife rescue boats were already on scene when we arrived, along with several Hamilton County Sheriff's deputies, two fire trucks and an ambulance. On the water, I could see what appeared to be a thirty-foot cabin cruiser listing heavily to starboard, black smoke pouring from its engine compartment.

"What's the situation?" Kate asked the Wildlife captain in charge of the rescue operation.

"Single occupant, male, approximately fifty years old. We pulled him out of the water about ten minutes ago. He's alive but unconscious. He doesn't seem to be injured, but it's possible he's suffering from smoke inhalation, maybe even hypothermia. The paramedics are working on him now."

I walked over to where the rescued man was being treated by paramedics. Even unconscious and soaking wet, I recognized him from the photographs in Drake's investigative files.

"It's Captain Marsh," I told Kate. "According to Jones' records, he's another boat operator who's been dumping for Ashcroft Chemical."

"So, another victim of the cover-up, or his boat accidentally caught fire," Kate said. "I'm betting it was the former."

The paramedic working on Marsh looked up as we approached.

"How's he doing?" I asked.

"He's stable, but he's got serious smoke inhalation. We need to get him to the hospital immediately."

"Can he talk?" Kate asked.

"Not right now. Maybe in a few hours if we're lucky."

As the ambulance carrying Marsh pulled away, Kate received a call from Agent Rebecca Mornay.

"Captain Gazzara, I'm at your police department with my EPA team," Mornay said. "We need to talk. I've been reviewing the environmental evidence you sent me, and we need to coordinate our response immediately."

"I'm sorry, ma'am, but we're dealing with multiple attempted and actual murders," Kate replied. "Someone just tried to kill another boat operator."

"Which is why I'm calling," Mornay said. "We've been in contact with federal law enforcement about establishing a joint task force. We're treating this as domestic terrorism."

———

An hour later, Kate and I were sitting in the police department's largest conference room with what seemed like half the federal government. Agent Rebecca Mornay had brought three EPA specialists, and there were two senior county deputies, two FBI agents and a representative from the Tennessee Bureau of Investigation.

"Let me begin by putting this in perspective," Mornay said, spreading satellite images across the conference table. "The environmental damage documented in Dr. Parker's research and corroborated by Dr. Jones' files represents one of the most alarming cases of industrial contamination we've ever investigated in the Southeast."

FBI SAIC Special Agent Collins leaned forward. "And the methods being used to cover it up—murder, attempted bombings—suggest we're dealing with an organization that has significant resources and connections."

Chief Johnston looked overwhelmed by the federal presence. "What exactly are you proposing?" he asked.

"We convene a joint task force," Collins replied. "We—that is the FBI—provide investigative resources and tactical support; EPA handles the environmental evidence and cleanup; TBI assists with state-level jurisdictional issues."

"And local police?" Kate asked, her tone carefully neutral.

"Essential," Mornay said diplomatically. "You know the local players, you've built relationships with witnesses, and you understand the community dynamics of what we're dealing with."

I could see Kate weighing the pros and cons. Federal resources versus loss of control. Protection for witnesses versus bureaucratic delays.

"What about operational control?" she asked.

"Shared command structure," Collins said. "Daily briefings, coordinated operations, joint decision-making on major moves."

"That sounds like federal control with local consultation," I observed.

Agent Jiminez, Collins' younger partner, spoke up. "Mr. Starke, we're trying to prevent more murders while building a case that will hold up in federal court. That requires coordination and proper procedures."

"Proper procedures haven't kept Dr. Parker, Dr. Jones, Drake, Muldoon, or Eddie Marsh from being targeted," Kate said. "These people are killing witnesses, or trying to, faster than we can protect them."

TBI Colonel Hayes spread out a tactical map. "Which is why we need to move quickly but carefully. We've identified at least three more potential targets based on the financial records you've uncovered."

"Three more boat operators?" I asked, frowning.

"Two boat operators and a laboratory technician who's been providing chemical analysis services," Jiminez replied. "All of them have been receiving payments from Ashcroft Chemical's shell companies."

Kate's phone buzzed with a text message. She glanced at it and her expression darkened.

"Problem?" I asked.

"It's from TJ," she said. "He says there's unusual activity at the old Ashcroft Chemical plant."

Collins snapped his head around to look at her. "What kind of activity?"

"Multiple vehicles, people moving equipment," she replied. "I'd say they're feeling the heat and are shutting the operation down. Moving materials and equipment out of the facility."

Mornay and Collins exchanged glances. "We need surveillance on that location immediately," Collins said. "If they're destroying evidence..."

"They're probably destroying more than evidence," I said. "They might be eliminating the entire operation and anyone who knows about it."

Colonel Hayes was already on his radio coordinating with Tennessee Wildlife officers who had boats on the river. "We can get eyes on the facility within twenty minutes," he said.

"What about the boat operators who might be targeted?" Kate asked.

"We'll put them in protective custody," Collins replied. "Federal marshals can have them secured within hours."

"What about Muldoon?" I asked. "He was supposed to make another dumping run tomorrow night."

"The sting operation is off," Collins replied. "After the bombing attempt, we moved him to a federal safe house. He's still cooperating, but we can't risk exposing him to another assassination attempt."

"So we lose the chance to document an actual dumping operation," Kate said.

"We have enough evidence from his previous testimony and Jones' documentation," Agent Mornay said. "The EPA doesn't need to see another illegal dump to build our case."

"Plus," Collins added, "if Victoria's people are willing to plant bombs, a sting operation would be too dangerous for everyone involved."

"We need to get teams to that location immediately," Collins said. "If they're destroying evidence, we need to stop them."

"How long for federal tactical response?" Johnston asked.

"Minimum two hours for proper coordination," Collins replied.

"In two hours, they'll have destroyed everything," Johnston said firmly. "I can have SWAT there in thirty minutes. This is still happening in my jurisdiction."

Collins looked uncomfortable. "Chief, this is a federal operation—"

"Then federalize it after we secure the evidence," Johnston shot back.

"Colonel Hayes, can the Wildlife officers establish surveillance immediately?" Kate asked.

"Already coordinating," Hayes replied. "We'll have eyes on the facility within twenty minutes."

"Good," Johnston said, putting down his phone. "SWAT

rolls in thirty. We'll hand it over to federal authorities once the scene is secure."

Chief Johnston leaned back in his chair. "So we're coordinating a federal environmental terrorism investigation from my conference room. Never thought I'd see the day," he said, with a wicked barracuda-like smile on his lips.

———

AN HOUR LATER, we were standing in the empty parking lot of the old Ashcroft Chemical facility, staring at what had once been a bustling operation but was now just another abandoned industrial site.

"They cleaned it out," SWAT Commander Riley reported to Johnston. "Professional job. At first look, there's nothing left. No equipment, no materials, no personnel. Just some tire tracks and oil stains to show anyone was ever here."

Kate and I walked through the main building with Agents Collins and Mornay. The concrete floors showed signs of recent activity—scuff marks from heavy equipment being moved, chemical stains that could have been from legitimate industrial processes, and the lingering smell of cleaning solvents.

"How long ago?" Collins asked.

"Based on the oil stains and tire impressions, most of the heavy stuff was gone days ago," Mike Willis said, whom Johnston had ordered in with his team along with the two SWAT teams, "but some of the tire tracks are fresh, and there's plenty of them, some less than an hour old, most at least six to eight hours. I'd say they finished up just before we got here."

Agent Mornay was taking water samples from various locations, but her expression wasn't optimistic. "Whatever they were storing here, they cleaned up after themselves pretty thoroughly. I'm finding trace chemicals, but nothing that wouldn't be expected in a decommissioned chemical plant."

We found three workers still on site when SWAT arrived—all carrying legitimate identification and work orders for "routine facility maintenance and equipment removal." Their story was simple and consistent: they'd been hired by a contracting company to clean out old equipment and prepare the site for potential sale.

"The company called us on Tuesday morning, early," the foreman said, a heavily tanned man named Mapin who seemed genuinely confused by all the law enforcement attention. "They said they needed the place cleaned out fast because they had a potential buyer. We've been working here ever since."

Kate interviewed the workers while I examined their paperwork. Everything looked legitimate—proper work orders, insurance documentation, even receipts for equipment rental.

"What kind of equipment were you removing?" Kate asked.

"Old chemical tanks, some pumps, laboratory equipment that had been sitting here for years," Mapin replied. "Nothing special. Most of it went to scrap metal dealers or hazardous waste disposal."

"Where?" Collins demanded.

Mapin consulted his clipboard. "Three different companies. I can give you the addresses, but they're all legitimate operations. We use them all the time for industrial cleanup jobs."

Collins immediately dispatched agents to check the

disposal companies, but I had a feeling they'd find the same thing we'd found here—legitimate businesses with proper documentation and no knowledge of illegal activities.

TJ approached me with a frustrated expression. "Harry, I watched them load truck after truck all morning. They knew exactly what they were doing. They were working in teams, everything coordinated, no wasted motion."

All I could do was shake my head.

By late afternoon, it was obvious that whoever had been running the illegal dumping operation had successfully erased nearly all evidence of their activities. The disposal companies checked out as legitimate, the workers' stories held up under questioning, and the physical evidence was minimal.

"They played us," Collins said grimly as we prepared to leave the facility. "Someone tipped them off that we were getting close, and they executed a complete shutdown."

"Or they were already planning to shut down after the bombing attempt on Muldoon," Kate suggested. "Maybe they decided the operation was getting too hot."

Chief Johnston looked around the empty facility with disgust. "So we've got nothing. No evidence, no arrests, no smoking gun."

"We've got confirmation that there was a major operation here," Agent Mornay said. "The chemical traces, the equipment marks, the coordination required for this kind of cleanup, it proves Dr. Parker and Dr. Jones were right about the illegal dumping."

"But it doesn't tell us who was running it," I said. "And it doesn't help us catch the people who killed Parker and Jones, or attempted the murders of Drake, Marsh and Muldoon."

————

THURSDAY AFTERNOON BROUGHT another development that reminded us how dangerous our investigation had become. Kate and I were back at the joint task force command center —the PD conference room—reviewing the disappointing raid results when my phone rang with a call from Amanda.

"Harry, I'm at Erlanger Hospital," she said, her voice tense. "Captain Marsh regained consciousness, and he's asking to speak with local police. He won't talk to the federal agents."

"Yeah, I know," I said, looking at Collins. "The feds want to control access to the witnesses."

"This man is terrified," Amanda continued. "He says he'll only talk to the investigators he's seen on the news covering the aquarium murders. He doesn't trust the federal authorities."

After some negotiation, Collins agreed to let Kate and me interview Marsh with Agent Jiminez present as an observer. "But nothing gets released to the media without task force approval," he insisted as we left.

The drive to Erlanger Hospital gave Jiminez another opportunity to lecture us about federal procedures, though I noticed he kept checking his phone nervously, like he was expecting bad news.

Captain Eddie Marsh looked exactly like what he was: a working-class boat operator who'd gotten in over his head with dangerous people. He was in his early fifties, weathered and bandaged, and his eyes immediately went to Agent Jiminez's federal credentials when we entered his room.

"I said local cops only," Marsh said, his voice hoarse.

"Agent Jiminez is here as an observer," Kate explained diplomatically. "I'm Captain Gazzara, this is Harry Starke. We're investigating the murders."

Marsh relaxed slightly. "Yeah, I seen you on the news, both

of you. Ask the right questions about what's been happening on the river and I'll do my best to answer them."

"We think whoever's behind the dumping tried to kill you today," I said directly.

"Wasn't no accident," Marsh confirmed immediately. "Someone put something in my fuel line. Made the engine catch fire when I started her up."

Kate took out her notebook. "Mr. Marsh, we know you've been transporting materials for what you thought were legitimate waste disposal operations. We need you to tell us everything you know."

"Lady, I don't think you understand what you're dealing with," Marsh said quietly. "These people don't just fire you when you become inconvenient. I seen what happened to Wiley Jones."

"Which is why we need your testimony to stop them," I said. "The task force can protect you, but we need to know who we're protecting you from."

After an hour of careful questioning, Marsh provided details that corroborated our other witnesses. The same woman—Victoria Ashcroft, we thought but couldn't confirm—had hired him four years ago. The same coordination with dam schedules, the same sealed containers, the same remote discharge points.

But Marsh also provided new information that troubled me.

"Last few months, it wasn't just the woman giving instructions," he said. "There was this other person, someone who seemed to know a lot about the river operations but wasn't part of the original setup."

"Can you describe this person?" Agent Jiminez asked, speaking for the first time.

"Never saw them clearly. Always met at night, always kept to the shadows. But they knew details about the dumping locations that even Victoria didn't seem to know. Like they was part of the operation, only not, if you get my meaning."

Kate and I exchanged glances. Me? I certainly got his meaning, but I didn't know what it meant.

As we left the hospital, my phone buzzed with a call from TJ. I put him on speaker.

"Harry, the disposal companies the workers mentioned; they all checked out. They're all legitimate, all have proper documentation for the equipment they received. It's a dead end."

"So whoever planned this cleanup thought of everything," Kate said.

"Yup, that's about the size of it," TJ replied.

8

Hidden Depths

Monday, Week 3

THE WEEKEND HAD PASSED QUIETLY ON THE SURFACE, BUT I could feel the undercurrents of frustration and growing danger. The failed raid at the Ashcroft Chemical plant had left everyone feeling like we'd been outmaneuvered by criminals who seemed to anticipate our every move. I spent some time with Amanda and Jade, played golf with my father, August, on Sunday morning, and we all had lunch at the club.

Kate called twice over the weekend, each time sounding more frustrated about witness protection issues and federal bureaucracy than before. By Monday morning of our third week, the consequences of that failed raid were becoming apparent in ways we hadn't anticipated.

I arrived at my office just after eight AM to find Jacque already at her desk, sorting through what appeared to be several days' worth of accumulated paperwork and phone messages.

I hadn't seen much of her or my office over the past couple of weeks and could see by the look on her face how frustrated she must be. She stood up and said, "About time you graced us with your presence. I have paperwork to—" She saw the grin, then shook her head, not bothering to hide her Jamaican accent, "Oh, what de hell. I give up." Despite being only thirty years old, Jacque had a presence that made her seem older and more experienced than her years. Her skin seemed to glow under the fluorescent lights, and her bushy black hair was pulled back in what she called her "serious business" style. She was wearing a charcoal gray business suit that somehow managed to look both professional and slightly rebellious— typical Jacque.

"So, Good marnin', Harry," she said, "and you look like hell, by de way. When was de last time you got a full night's sleep?"

"Good morning to you too, Jacque," I replied, "I need coffee. You want some?"

She shook her head, so I went on through to the break- room and poured myself coffee from the pot she'd already prepared. The fact that it was perfectly brewed, exactly the way I liked it, was just another example of how well she knew my habits. "And I've been sleeping fine, thank you very much," I said as she followed me in.

She looked up at me with those sharp brown eyes that missed nothing, and I could see the skepticism written clearly across her face. "Right. And I suppose those dark circles under your eyes are from too much readin'," she said as she handed me a manila folder. "These are the calls you need to return today. The red tabs are urgent, yellow are routine, and the green ones are reporters who want to know when you're planning to solve this case."

I flipped through the messages. "Reporters are still calling?"

"Channel 7 wants to know if Amanda's reporting creates a conflict of interest. The Times Free Press is asking about the failed raid at the chemical plant. And the other three media outlets want to know if the environmental terrorism angle is being covered up." She paused, consulting another notepad. "Oh, and your father called. He wants to know if you need legal representation."

"What? August called? Why would I need legal representation?"

"He seemed concerned about the political pressure angle," she replied. "He said something about making sure you don't get scapegoated if this case goes sideways." Jacque's expression became more serious. "Harry, he might have a point. From what I can see, there are a lot of powerful people who want this investigation to disappear."

"Environmental terrorism? Who's calling it that?" I asked as she followed me to my office, knowing it hadn't been released to the press yet... or had it?

"Everyone after that federal task force meeting Thursday. Word gets around, Harry. People are nervous about what this all means for the Tennessee River, for the aquarium, for the city's environmental reputation."

I had to admit, Jacque's assessment was probably accurate.

"What's your read on where we stand after that raid disaster?" I asked.

"Honestly? I think whoever you're chasing played you perfectly," she said, settling into the seat across from my desk.

"They cleaned out that facility so thoroughly it was like they knew exactly when you were coming."

"You think they're getting inside information?" I asked.

"They have to be. Harry, think about the timing. The cleanup crews were already finishing up when SWAT arrived. That's not luck; that's advance warning." She reached down and took a yellow legal pad covered with her beautiful cursive handwriting from her bag. "I've been thinking about this all weekend, and the more I analyze it, the more convinced I am that someone with access to your so-called task force tipped them off."

I sipped my coffee, considering her analysis. It was a possibility that had been nagging at me since Thursday's disappointment.

"So someone tipped them off," I muttered, leaning back in my chair, staring up at the ceiling.

"Or someone's been monitoring your communications," she said. "Either way, whoever it is has access to operational intelligence."

My phone buzzed with a call from Kate.

"Kate. What's up?"

"There's been a development, and it's not good news. We need to meet."

"What kind of development?" I asked, leaning forward and grabbing a pen.

"The kind we should discuss in person," she replied. "Can you be here in thirty minutes? And Harry, bring Tim with you. We're going to need his help."

"On my way," I said as I rose to my feet.

As I gathered my jacket, Jacque, now also on her feet, handed me another file. "This is the research on the shell companies Tim identified. I cross-referenced them with

Hamilton County political donation records and came up with some very interesting patterns."

I glanced at the file. It was, as always, meticulously organized—Jacque's trademark. Color-coded tabs, detailed summaries, and what looked like a complex flowchart showing relationships between companies and politicians.

"Interesting, you say?"

"Very interesting. Ashcroft Chemical and its subsidiaries have been major donors to several local political campaigns over the past five years. City council, county commission, even some judicial races. It all looks like influence-buying, Harry. And Harry, some of the biggest recipients have been the same officials who've been pressuring Chief Johnston to limit the investigation." She took back the file and flipped to a specific page covered with financial data. "Look at these numbers."

"Just give me the facts, Jacque. Anyone specific?"

"Councilman Bradley, who called you and Kate's work a 'vendetta,' has received over thirty thousand dollars from Ashcroft-related companies. County Commissioner Walsh, who complained about 'wasting taxpayer money,' got twenty-five thousand. And there are others."

She handed me the file, and I stared at the numbers. "How did you get access to campaign finance records?"

"It's easy enough; public information," she replied. "Most people just don't bother to look for patterns, and when they do, they don't cross-reference databases." She smiled. "Isn't that what you pay me for, among other things? Plus, I still have contacts from my graduate program who know how to access and analyze this kind of data."

"Yes, that's what I pay you for," I said. "Jacque, I need you to keep digging into these political connections." I handed her the file. "Find out who else might have financial relationships with Ashcroft Chemical. And see if you can identify any patterns in the timing of the donations versus policy decisions."

"Already working on it," she replied. "I've got requests pending for records from the state ethics commission and the county clerk's office. I'll have a complete analysis by this afternoon, including a timeline showing donations correlated with votes on environmental issues."

———

TWENTY-FIVE MINUTES LATER, I was sitting in the joint command center with Tim, who'd taken a seat in the corner of the room, Kate, Agent Collins, and Agent Mornay, listening to news that confirmed my worst fears about the consequences of Thursday's failed raid.

"Our three protected witnesses have all asked to be released from federal custody," Collins said grimly. "We moved Muldoon, Marsh, and the lab technician to safe houses over the weekend. They're scared, Harry. Really scared."

"Why?" Kate asked, though I could see from her expression that she already suspected the answer.

"They're terrified," Collins said, "because after learning how thoroughly the chemical plant was cleaned out, they don't believe we can protect them from people with that level of organization and resources. Muldoon specifically said he'd rather take his chances on his own than trust federal protection."

Agent Mornay spread out some crime scene photographs. "And they may be right to be scared. There's been another death. Hamilton County Commissioner Ralph Walsh was found dead in his home office Sunday morning. An apparent heart attack, according to the initial assessment."

I remembered the name from Jacque's research. "Walsh was receiving campaign donations from Ashcroft Chemical," I said. "And he's been one of the county officials pressuring the chief to limit the scope of the environmental investigation. Where is he, by the way?"

The chief must have been reading my mind, because the conference room door opened and Johnston walked in, and he wasn't looking happy. He was frowning, and there were stress lines around his eyes that I'd not seen before. Not that I saw him very often.

"Sorry I'm late," he said, taking his seat at the head of the table. "I've been on the phone with the mayor's office, the county commission chairman, and three different reporters in the past hour." He looked around the room. "What did I miss?"

"We were just discussing Commissioner Walsh," Kate said.

Johnston's expression darkened as he looked at me and said, "Ralph Walsh is dead, Harry."

"I know," I replied, "and I think something stinks. I'm also thinking he was another loose end."

"Either that or it's a coincidence," Collins said.

Coincidence? I thought. *Are you kidding me?* "You want to tell us about it, Kate?" I asked.

Kate nodded, consulted her notes, and said, "His wife found him at his desk Sunday morning. He'd been working late Saturday night on what she described as 'city business.' There were no signs of struggle, no evidence of a break-in, nothing obviously suspicious. The scene looked like a man who'd simply had a heart attack while working late."

"Except for the timing," I observed. "And what d'you want to bet Hensley finds an injection point behind his ear?"

"Exactly," Kate said. "We have a corrupt official with financial ties to Ashcroft Chemical dies of an apparent heart attack just days after two boating incidents and a major raid at the chemical plant." Kate flipped through her notebook. "And according to his wife, Walsh had been acting nervous and distracted all last week. She said he'd been making and receiving phone calls at odd hours, and he'd been asking questions about family finances and legal protections."

"Sounds like someone who was reconsidering his options," Agent Mornay observed.

"That's what we think," Collins agreed. "And if they thought there was even a doubt of Walsh's loyalty, that would be reason enough to eliminate him."

Agent Mornay leaned forward. "Here's what concerns us. The timing and precision of Walsh's death suggest the killer has access to real-time intelligence about our investigation."

"What do you mean?" Kate asked.

I almost laughed out loud. It was exactly what I'd been thinking only an hour earlier.

"Walsh died Saturday night," Collins replied. "But according to our records, we didn't identify him as a person of interest until Friday afternoon when we analyzed the political donation records. The killer—if that's what happened— moved on him within twenty-four hours of us flagging him as potentially corrupt."

I leaned back in my chair and surveyed the room, but said nothing.

"We're saying someone knew Walsh was compromised before we even approached him," Mornay said grimly. "Which means they either have access to our communications, our databases, or someone with access to our investigation is compromised."

The room fell silent as the implications sank in. Johnston's face had gone pale, and I could see him mentally reviewing everyone who'd had access to case information.

With tongue in cheek, I inwardly shook my head. *This is exactly what happens when you get too many people and agencies involved,* I thought.

"It appears to be methodical," Kate said. "Someone's working through a list."

"But who has access to that kind of information?" Collins asked. "Who would know exactly which officials were corrupt, which witnesses needed to be eliminated, which boat operators posed a threat?"

"And that's the real question, isn't it?" I said. "It has to be someone with inside knowledge of both the criminal network and the investigation." I looked across the room. "Tim?"

Tim had been sitting quietly in the corner, hunched over his laptop with an intense focus that meant he was deep into some kind of data analysis. He looked up, pushed his glasses further up the bridge of his nose, and blinked twice like he was refocusing on the real world.

"Um, er, yeah. So, I've been monitoring digital communications and financial transactions related to Commissioner Walsh's death," he said, his fingers still hovering over the keyboard as if he might dive back into the data at any moment. "Something's not right about the timing and circumstances."

"And who are you?" Mornay asked.

"Tim's my IT expert," I explained. "Captain Gazzara requested his presence."

Mornay looked a little put out, but continued, "What d'you mean, not right?"

I smiled and looked away. Mornay was obviously unfamiliar with Tim's habit of making dramatic statements without explanation.

Tim pushed his glasses with his finger again, a nervous tick that became more pronounced when he had an audience of strangers. "Walsh received a phone call Saturday evening from a number that traces back to a burner phone," he said. "The call lasted two minutes eleven seconds, and it was the last incoming communication to his house before his death."

Kate leaned forward. "Any idea who called him, Tim?"

"No, but I can tell you that the same burner phone has been used to contact other officials who've received Ashcroft Chemical donations. Always brief calls, always in the evening, always within a few days of significant developments in your investigation." Tim's fingers started tapping silently on the table, another sign that his mind was racing ahead of his words.

"You think someone's been coordinating with corrupt officials," I said.

"Or warning them," Tim replied. "But there's something else. Walsh's computer shows that on Saturday night he was researching witness protection programs and federal plea bargain procedures. Like he was considering cooperating with law enforcement."

Agent Collins immediately sat up straighter. "Wait a minute. How exactly did you gain access to Commissioner Walsh's personal computer?"

Tim froze, his fingers stopping mid-tap on the table. He glanced at me, then back at Collins, pushing his glasses up nervously. "Well, I... that is... his home network wasn't exactly... secure."

"Are you telling me you hacked into a dead county

commissioner's computer?" Collins' tone was that of a federal agent who was not amused.

"I prefer to think of it as... unauthorized access for investigative purposes," Tim said, looking increasingly uncomfortable. "The man's dead, and we needed to know if his death was connected to our case."

Chief Johnston rubbed his forehead. "Good grief, Tim, do you have any idea what kind of legal problems that could create?"

"Oh, for Pete's sake," I said. "He's on our side, Chief. And he works for me. If there are legal problems, they're mine to deal with. Let's get on with this, shall we, before someone else has to die."

Collins and Mornay exchanged glances, then looked at the chief, who was seated with his arms folded, glowering at me. I winked at him. It didn't go down well.

Collins shook his head slowly. "Mr. Starke, we'll need to discuss the admissibility issues this creates for any evidence derived from that computer access."

"And we'll need documentation of exactly what was accessed and when," Mornay added, looking distinctly uncomfortable. "The defense attorneys are going to have a field day with this."

"Noted," I said. "But right now, we have a dead county commissioner and a pattern of murders. Are we going to let legal technicalities stop us from catching the killer?"

Collins looked like he wanted to argue further, but apparently decided the information was too valuable to ignore. "Fine. But from now on, all computer access goes through proper legal channels."

"Again, noted!" I snapped. "Now, can we get on with it?"

"So," Collins said, after a few seconds of deliberation,

"Walsh might have been killed to prevent him from turning state's evidence."

"That's my theory," Tim agreed, still a little nervous. I nodded at him and smiled, and he continued, "And if I'm right, it means someone's monitoring not just the investigation, but also the corrupt officials who might be tempted to save themselves by cooperating."

"Has the autopsy been completed?" I asked, changing the subject.

Kate checked her phone. "Dr. Hensley's scheduled to perform it this afternoon. We should have preliminary results by this evening."

"If Walsh was murdered, how was it done?" Agent Mornay asked. "The initial assessment was natural causes."

"That's what we need to find out," Kate said. "But if it follows the pattern we've seen with Dr. Parker and Dr. Jones..."

"Tetrodotoxin injection designed to look like natural death," I finished.

"Which would mean the same killer is responsible," Collins observed.

Duh! I couldn't help but think.

As the afternoon progressed, we finally received confirmation of what we'd suspected. Dr. Hensley called Kate just after five o'clock with the autopsy results.

"Commissioner Walsh died of an injection of tetrodotoxin injection," she said without preamble. "Same as the other victims. I found a small puncture wound behind the left ear. I'll send the full report as soon as I've finished it." And with that, she hung up.

"So, now we know it's the same killer," I said, "the question then becomes, is this killer working for Victoria Ashcroft or against her?"

Kate looked up from her notes. "What do you mean?"

"Think about it. If Victoria hired someone to eliminate witnesses, why would they also kill corrupt officials who were helping her? Walsh was pressuring us to limit the investigation. He was useful to her."

"Unless the killer has their own agenda," Collins said slowly.

"Or unless someone's cleaning house to protect a larger operation," Agent Mornay suggested.

A couple of hours later, as evening fell, I was back in my office with Jacque, reviewing the day's developments and trying to make sense of the evolving pattern. She'd spread out charts, timelines, and financial records across the conference table, creating what looked like a complex murder investigation board.

"Three murders, all with the same method, all connected to the Ashcroft Chemical conspiracy," I said, summarizing what we'd learned.

"But different types of victims," Jacque observed, pointing to her analysis. "Dr. Parker was a threat to expose the crimes. Dr. Jones was an inside informant who knew too much. Commissioner Walsh was a corrupt official who might have been ready to cooperate with law enforcement."

"You're saying you don't think the killer is just eliminating threats to Victoria Ashcroft?" I asked. "But what else could they be doing?"

"I'm saying the killer might be eliminating threats to themselves. Harry, what if someone else was involved in the conspiracy, someone who's now removing anyone who could implicate them?" She tapped the timeline she'd created. "Look at the pattern. Each murder eliminates a different type of threat, but they all point to the same objective: protecting someone's identity."

It was a disturbing possibility that I hadn't fully considered. "A partner or competitor... maybe?" I asked.

"Or someone who was supposed to be investigating the crimes but was actually enabling them," she said quietly. "I mean, we already believe someone's leaking information. That means we have a corrupt member of the task force. What if—"

"That person is now eliminating everyone who could expose their involvement," I finished for her, understanding where her logic was leading.

The implications hit me like a physical blow. I sat back in my chair, my mind racing through the possibilities. *Someone with a badge, someone we trusted*. I thought about the failed raid at the chemical plant, how perfectly timed the cleanup had been. The systematic elimination of witnesses who could connect the dots. The political pressure that seemed to anticipate our investigation before we even knew where it was heading.

"Geez, Jacque," I muttered, running a hand through my hair. "If you're right, we've been playing poker with someone who can see our cards."

"Exactly," she said. "A corrupt law enforcement official would have access to both sides. They'd know who the criminals are, and they'd know what the investigation has discovered. They could eliminate anyone who threatens to expose their double game."

"It would explain a lot," I muttered. "The advance warning, the perfect timing, the political coordination. Someone's been orchestrating this from the inside."

"And now that the federal task force is involved, that person is running out of time and options," Jacque continued. "Which makes them exponentially more dangerous."

I shook my head; it was almost unbelievable. If someone in law enforcement had been compromised, it would explain how the criminals had stayed ahead of our investigation, how they'd known about the raid in advance, and how they'd managed to eliminate witnesses, or in the cases of Marsh and Muldoon, tried to.

"Jacque, I need you to research something else for me, please. Find out which officials, law enforcement officers, or regulatory inspectors have had financial relationships with Ashcroft Chemical or its subsidiaries."

"Good thinking, Harry," she replied.

"I'm also thinking that someone with official access has been providing information to protect the dumping operation. And now that the investigation has gotten too close to the truth, that person might be eliminating anyone who could expose their involvement." I studied her timeline, noting the methodical progression of murders. "It has to be someone with inside knowledge of law enforcement procedures and investigative techniques," I muttered. "It has to be."

"That introduces a terrifying scenario," Jacque said softly. "Because if you're right, it means the killer knows exactly what you're doing, when you're doing it, where you're going, and who you're talking to."

A terrifying scenario indeed, I thought.

9

Toxic Legacy

Tuesday

NEEDLESS TO SAY, I HAD ANOTHER RESTLESS NIGHT, TOSSING and turning as my mind wrestled with the implications of Commissioner Walsh's murder and the systematic nature of the killings we were investigating. By five-thirty AM, I gave up on sleep and decided to go for a run along East Brow Road.

The morning air was crisp, with a hint of fog over the mountaintop. As I ran the familiar route, returning along West Brow Road, I continued to mull things over with little to no result. Frustrating? You have no idea.

I returned home, showered, dressed in jeans, a white Tee and black leather jacket, and then drove to my father's home where I found Amanda was up and dressed and making coffee while Jade sat at the kitchen table working on what appeared to be a coloring book.

"You're up early," Amanda said, handing me a cup of coffee. "Bad night?"

"Couldn't shut my brain off," I replied, kissing her cheek. "Bogies in the dark corners of the ceiling, and my mind. Too many pieces of this case that don't quite fit together."

Amanda set down scrambled eggs and toast for all of us. "Speaking of which," she said as she sat down, "I've been doing some background research on the Ashcroft family for a follow-up story. Did you know there are some really interesting patterns in their business history?"

"Oh yeah, what kind of patterns?" I asked.

"Well, for one, take Victoria's father," she began. "The timing of William Ashcroft's death and the subsequent changes in company operations. According to my sources, Ashcroft Chemical became much more profitable almost immediately after Victoria took over."

"Really?" I said after swallowing a mouthful of scrambled egg. "How much more profitable?"

"Dramatically. Their revenue increased by sixty percent in the first two years after her father died. That's unusual for a company that had been struggling with environmental compliance issues."

I thought about the dumping operation. "Unless they suddenly found a way to eliminate their biggest expense," I said.

"Environmental compliance and waste disposal costs," Amanda agreed. "If they stopped properly disposing of chemical waste and started dumping it illegally..."

"They'd save millions, and thus the company would

become much more profitable," I finished. "Amanda, that's exactly the kind of motive that leads to murder."

Jade looked up from her coloring again. "Are you talking about the bad guys again?"

"Just a little bit," I said. "But we're almost done."

Amanda lowered her voice. "Harry, there's something else. I've also been looking into Victoria's personal background, and she has connections that go way beyond Chattanooga business circles."

"Go on," I said, then took a bite of toast.

"The defense industry, military contractors, and even some federal agencies. She's served on advisory boards and consulting committees that deal with the environmental cleanup of military facilities."

Now that's information worth pursuing, I thought

"And if she's been using those connections to acquire and dispose of materials illegally..." she trailed off, took a sip of her coffee, then looked at me, her beautiful green eyes glistening. "What d'you think, Harry?"

"I think you're on a winner," I said. "But you need to be careful. These people are killers."

She nodded. "I keep Maria close."

"That may not be enough," I said. "She's good, but... just be careful, okay?"

As I prepared to leave for the office, Amanda handed me another cup of coffee for the road. "Harry, *you be* careful today. If Victoria Ashcroft has the kind of connections I think she does, she's more dangerous than you might realize."

"I know," I replied. "But we're getting close to exposing what she's been doing. And once we do, her connections won't be able to protect her." *But are we getting close?* I couldn't help but wonder.

I arrived in my office by eight that morning and immediately got stuck into reviewing the growing stack of evidence that painted an increasingly disturbing picture of systematic corruption and murder. The coffee was strong, Jacque was already deep into her research, and my phone had been mercifully quiet for the first hour of the day. And then the peace ended when Kate called at just after nine.

"How was your night?" she asked by way of an opener.

"Rough," I replied. "How about you?"

"Same," she said. "I called because I've been reviewing Dr. Parker's computer models. They are way more extensive than we initially realized, and they show predictions that are... well, let's just say they're catastrophic. Harry, the pollution could have a devastating effect on the river and cost the city millions in cleanup and lawsuits. Can you meet me at UTC? Dr. Howard has agreed to walk us through Parker's research."

"Yep, I can be there in thirty minutes," I replied, then, "Kate, I need a favor. I'm worried about Amanda and Jade. Maria is good, but she's only one person. Can you—"

"Consider it done," she said, cutting me off. "I'll assign an officer immediately. I'll call and tell her to be expecting him. That good?"

"Thanks, Kate. They're staying with August. I'll see you in thirty minutes."

———

I FOUND Kate and Samson waiting for me outside the Environmental Sciences building. The big German Shepherd looked alert and was obviously in a happy mood, which usually meant Kate wasn't expecting trouble. Yet.

"These computer models; what exactly are we talking about?" I asked as we walked toward the building.

"According to Dr. Howard, Dr. Parker had been building predictive models for over a year. She was projecting long-term ecological damage."

We found Dr. Sally Howard in her office, surrounded by computer printouts, charts, and what appeared to be complex mathematical models that only a scientist could understand. She looked tired, as if she hadn't been sleeping well, but her eyes were sharp and focused.

"Thank you for coming," she said, gesturing for us to sit. "I've been going through more of Jennifer's backup files, and I found something that I think might explain why someone would kill to keep this information secret."

She turned her computer monitor toward us, showing a series of graphs and projections that looked like something from a disaster movie.

"Jennifer's models show that the chemical contamination in the Tennessee River system has reached critical levels in several areas," she explained. "But more importantly, she'd identified the specific chemicals being dumped, and they're not just industrial waste."

"What do you mean?" Kate asked, frowning.

"Some of the compounds Jennifer identified are precursors to chemical weapons. Organophosphates, chlorinated compounds, heavy metals in combinations that suggest someone was either disposing of weapons manufacturing byproducts or actually testing chemical weapons development."

"Chemical weapons?" I muttered. "You're kidding!"

"Not at all," she replied. "Jennifer believed that whoever was dumping these materials had access to military or defense industry sources. The chemical signatures don't match typical industrial waste patterns."

Kate leaned forward. "Did she document where these materials were coming from?"

"She did," Sally said, pulling up another file. "She traced some of the chemical signatures to a decommissioned military research facility about fifty miles upstream from Chattanooga. The facility was supposedly cleaned up and sealed fifteen years ago."

"Fifteen years ago," I repeated. "Right around the time Victoria Ashcroft took over her father's company."

"Exactly," Sally replied. "And according to Jennifer's research, Ashcroft Chemical was one of the contractors involved in the cleanup of that military facility."

Kate and I exchanged glances. "So Victoria would have had access to materials that were supposed to be destroyed."

"Or disposed of safely," Sally said. "Instead, it looks like she may have been dumping them in the river."

Sally pulled up another file. "These are financial projections," she explained. "Jennifer calculated that proper disposal of these materials would have cost Ashcroft Chemical over fifty million dollars. By dumping them illegally, Victoria saved her company a fortune. And then there's this," she continued, bringing up yet another file, a note to Jennifer herself. "She found evidence that someone else had been investigating the chemical weapons connection. Someone with access to classified military records."

"Who?" I asked.

"She never found out. But according to her notes, this person had been trying to contact her for months. Whoever it was wanted to share information about the original military research and what was supposed to happen to the materials."

"Did they ever make contact?" Kate asked.

"Only by email and voicemail on her office phone. Just numbers—coordinates, dates, things like that."

"Do you have access to those messages or emails?" I asked.

"I saved everything I could access. But Jennifer was careful about security. She said she was worried about industrial espionage and electronic surveillance."

Sally led us to Dr. Parker's office, which had been resealed since the break-in but was still accessible with Sally's key. Samson entered first, casting around, nose twitching. Kate followed, then Sally, then me. The first thing I noticed was how different it felt: not just empty, but somehow violated by the search that had taken place.

"Jennifer hid backup drives in several locations," Sally said. "Your man Willis found most of them, but Jennifer was smart," she continued as she stepped over to an aquarium tank in the corner of the office. She pushed the sleeve of her right arm up above her elbow, reached down into the water, moved a piece of river rock, scratched around in the gravel and retrieved a small waterproof container. "Got it," she said triumphantly. "She knew a thorough search would reveal the obvious places like books and filing cabinets. But they missed this one," she said, as she opened the container and took out a thumbdrive.

"She was paranoid about someone stealing her research," she said, handing it to Kate, "so she made multiple copies and hid them in places only I would know to look."

Kate plugged the drive into Parker's computer, and within minutes we were looking at files that painted an even more horrible picture than even I'd imagined.

"Look at this," Kate said. "It's labeled Weapons Analysis.

Jennifer documented specific chemical compounds produced in military weapons research."

"And here," she said as I leaned in over her shoulder. "This one's about delivery systems, and it looks like someone was testing dispersal methods in the river system."

"Testing?" Sally's voice was barely above a whisper. "You mean they were using the river as a testing ground for chemical weapons?"

"According to these notes, yes," Kate said, and then read, "Small-scale dispersal tests, environmental impact studies, effectiveness measurements."

"Damn!" I muttered. "So Collins and company were right. It is environmental terrorism and, if what Dr. Parker says here is true, they were also testing weapons."

"Which explains why the federal task force got involved so quickly," Kate said. "They must have suspected the weapons connection."

"Or they already knew," I said.

And then, as if on cue, my phone buzzed with a call from Agent Collins. I answered it on speaker.

"Harry, we need you and Captain Gazzara here at the command center immediately."

"Why, what's up?" I asked, warily.

"Not over the phone, Harry," he replied. "How long before you can get here?"

"Twenty, thirty minutes," I replied.

"Make it twenty," Collins said and hung up.

Sally stared at us, biting her bottom lip, then said, "If they were testing chemical weapons in the river, how many people have been exposed? How much contamination is there?"

"Good questions," Kate replied, "to which we need answers. Dr. Howard, I need you to compile everything you have about Jennifer's weapons research and send it to me. Do not share it with anyone else. And I need a copy of this thumb drive, please. "

She nodded, reached into one of the desk drawers, took out another thumb drive, inserted it into an empty slot and then copied the files over. It took only a minute. She handed the drive to Kate who handed it to me and said, "See what Tim can make of it." Then she turned to Sally and said. "Stay safe. Don't talk to anyone you don't know, and maintain a gap of at least six feet between you and anyone you do talk to. Don't trust anyone."

But the surprises kept coming. As we left the university, Kate's radio crackled with a message from dispatch.

"Captain Gazzara, we have reports of a suspicious death in Hixson. Male victim, mid-forties, found in his car in the lot at the Riverwalk Marina. Preliminary assessment suggests possible carbon monoxide poisoning, but responding officers are requesting detective support."

Kate and I looked at each other. "Another boat captain?" she asked.

"Or someone else who knew too much about the dumping operation," I replied. "This is getting out of hand, Kate."

Twenty minutes later, we were standing next to a late-model Nissan Rogue, watching the medical examiner's team process what appeared to be another carefully planned murder disguised as an accident.

According to the driving license in his wallet, the victim was William Murdoch, age forty-four. He was slumped over the steering wheel with the engine running and the windows up. A garden hose had been attached to the exhaust pipe and fed through a partially opened rear window. It was the classic carbon monoxide poisoning setup.

"Looks like suicide," the responding officer said. "Guy probably couldn't handle the stress of whatever he was involved in."

I didn't answer at first. Neither did Kate. It took only a quick look for me to decide it was a homicide.

"Except suicide victims don't usually duct-tape the hose connections or position themselves so carefully," I said. "This was staged."

Kate was going through Murdoch's wallet. "William Murdoch, licensed environmental consultant. And look at this; he has business cards from three different waste disposal companies."

I thought for a moment. Something about what she said, the business cards, hit a nerve. "D'you think he could be Dr. Parker's mysterious contact?" I asked.

"That would make sense," she replied as Dr. Hensley approached.

"Whatcha got, Doc?" I asked.

She looked at me with obvious distain. I smiled benignly at her, which made her mood even worse.

"My preliminary assessment is carbon monoxide poisoning, of course," she said primly. "But there are some inconsistencies that concern me."

"Inconsistencies?" Kate asked.

"The positioning of the body, the lack of defensive wounds or signs of struggle, and the fact that the victim's hands are folded unnaturally in his lap."

"So what are you thinking?" Kate asked.

"Someone could have incapacitated him first, then staged the scene to look like carbon monoxide poisoning. And if this follows the pattern we've been seeing..."

"You'll find a tetrodotoxin injection site during the full autopsy," I finished.

She nodded, "This is getting old," she muttered. Then to Kate, "I'll call you when I know more."

As we were finishing up at the marina, my phone rang. It was Agent Collins, and boy was he pissed off.

"Where the hell are you?" he demanded. "We've been waiting for over an hour."

"We got called to a crime scene," Kate replied when I put him on speaker.

"Another death? Why didn't you call me immediately?"

"Because we needed to secure the scene and determine if it was actually connected," I said, trying to keep the irritation out of my voice. "It is. The victim is an environmental consultant named Murdoch."

"Damn!" Collins muttered. "Another one? How many more people are going to die while we're playing catch-up? Get back here now. It's important."

When we arrived back in the conference room some thirty minutes later to find Tim seated in his usual corner, his computer on his lap, and Collins, still angry, pacing back and forth behind the conference table like a caged animal. Agent Mornay looked equally frustrated, and there were several new faces in the room; federal agents I didn't recognize.

"Before you say anything," Collins said as we took our seats, "let me make something clear. From now on, all crime scenes get reported to this task force immediately. No independent investigation, no solo fact-finding missions. We're dealing with something much bigger than local murders, and we can't afford to have critical information scattered across different agencies."

"Understood," Kate said diplomatically, though I could see her jaw tightening. "Samson, sit! It's okay. Good boy."

Samson obviously didn't like Collins' attitude. His hackles were up, his head down and his ears flattened, but he did as he was told and lowered himself slowly down into sitting position at Kate's side. Collins glowered at her and the dog. Kate glared defiantly back him.

Me? I quietly texted Tim and asked him to do a deep dive into William Murdoch, our murder victim.

"You were saying," Kate said, glaring at Collins.

He took a deep breath, glanced again at Samson, who was watching him over the edge of the table, then said, "Yes, well. We've received classified information from the Defense Department that fifteen years ago, a military chemical research facility some fifty miles upstream from here was decommission, and that Ashcroft Chemical was one of the contractors hired to dispose of classified materials."

"And?" Kate asked, neglecting to tell him that we already knew about it.

"It seems not all of the materials were properly accounted for. Significant quantities of chemical weapons precursors were listed as 'disposed of' but may have been diverted instead."

Agent Mornay leaned forward. "We're talking about compounds used in nerve agents and chemical warfare research, materials that should have been destroyed under federal oversight."

"You're saying Victoria Ashcroft stole military chemical weapons?" I asked.

"We're saying someone with access to that cleanup operation has been in possession of classified military materials for fifteen years," Collins replied. "And if those materials ended up in the Tennessee River..."

"The consequences would be devastating," Kate finished.

"We've also been investigating the circumstances surrounding William Ashcroft's death fifteen years ago, and we've discovered some troubling information."

"What kind of information?" I asked.

"William Ashcroft contacted EPA investigators three weeks before his death," Collins replied. "He was planning to provide documentation about illegal disposal of military materials from the decommissioned research facility."

Kate leaned forward. "And then he conveniently died of a heart attack."

"That's what made us suspicious," Collins said. "So we reached out to a Dr. Richard Sheddon, who was the medical examiner at the time," Mornay said. "He remembers the case clearly."

"And?" Kate prompted.

"Dr. Sheddon said he'd wanted to do a full autopsy because something felt wrong about the scene, but Victoria Ashcroft insisted on immediate cremation for 'religious reasons.' She had legal authority as next of kin, and she pushed hard. Ashcroft was cremated within hours of the death."

"Before Doc could do proper toxicology tests," I said.

"Exactly," Collins agreed.

Collins pulled out another file and continued, "Combined with what we know about the current murders and Victoria's access to the military materials, we believe she killed her father to prevent him from exposing the illegal weapons disposal operation."

"We think Victoria Ashcroft killed William Ashcroft,"

Mornay said. "And has been systematically eliminating anyone who threatens to expose her operation ever since."

Mornay spread out architectural drawings. "We've also located the decommissioned treatment plant. Apparently, it's been serving as a base of operations. It contains laboratory equipment, holding cells, and what appears to be a sophisticated chemical processing operation."

"Holding cells?" Kate asked.

"Rooms that could be used to contain people temporarily. Soundproofed, reinforced, equipped with ventilation systems that could be used for... testing purposes."

"You're saying Victoria has been conducting human experiments?" I asked.

"We're saying the facility contains equipment and infrastructure that could support chemical weapons development and testing," Collins replied carefully. "Including capabilities for testing effects on living subjects."

"But you can't prove any of that," I stated.

Neither Collins nor Mornay answered.

"I thought not," I said, caustically.

As the afternoon progressed, Tim's analysis of Murdoch's business records and phone communications began to reveal his connection to the illegal dumping operation.

It was a little after three o'clock when Tim looked up at me, nodded and opened his eyes wide.

"Go ahead, Tim," I said.

He cleared his throat, glanced at Collins, and began, "Murdoch wasn't just any old environmental consultant. His company specialized in waste disposal documentation and environmental impact assessments for industrial clients—"

"What? Stop!" Collins snapped. "What are you doing?"

"I ran a background check on the murder victim," Tim replied.

"I thought I told you—"

"I told him to," I said. "It's a simple background check. We do it all the time. It's part of the job…" I trailed off, narrowed my eyes and continued, "Why would you object to that, Agent Collins?"

He obviously didn't like what I was inferring, because he looked round and told Tim to continue.

Tim coughed, cleared his throat again and said, "As I was saying—"

"You said industrial clients," Kate said, cutting him off again. "Does that include Ashcroft Chemical?" Kate asked.

"Including Ashcroft Chemical and several of its subsidiaries," Tim confirmed. "Murdoch's phone records show he'd been in contact with someone using the same burner phone that called Commissioner Walsh."

Collins leaned forward and I thought he was going to do it again. Instead, he said, "The same phone? Are you sure?"

Tim awarded him one of his looks, and I couldn't help but smile.

"Yeah, I'm sure," he replied. "And Murdoch's computer files show he was providing disposal certificates for materials that were never actually disposed of properly. Certificates that would satisfy regulatory inspections while the materials were actually being dumped illegally."

I could see that both Mornay and Collins were becoming increasingly uncomfortable, so I said, "So let's be clear. What you're saying is that Murdoch was providing the paperwork to cover the illegal dumping operation?"

"That's what it looks like," Tim agreed. "False documentation, fraudulent disposal certificates, fake environmental impact reports that covered up the real levels of contamination."

Agent Mornay nodded grimly. "Which makes him another person who could provide testimony about the scope of the criminal operation. No wonder he's dead."

But more importantly, Tim's analysis of Murdoch's phone records showed that he'd been in contact with someone using the same burner phone that had called Commissioner Walsh.

"It looks like someone's been coordinating with all the corrupt participants," Tim said. "Murdoch, Walsh, and probably others we haven't identified yet."

Chief Johnston, who had been listening quietly, finally spoke up. "So, someone, probably Victoria Ashcroft, has been dumping military grade chemicals in our river for more than fifteen years?"

"That's... basically what we're telling you, yes," Collins replied.

"Which is why this case is now classified as a matter of national security," Agent Mornay said. "And why we need to speed up our investigation before more people are killed."

I heaved a sigh, sat back in my chair and stared at Tim. He gave me a toothy grin, which didn't make me feel any better or any more confident.

Later that afternoon, back in my own office, Jacque and I were trying to process the magnitude of what we'd discovered.

"Chemical weapons testing in the Tennessee River," she said, shaking her head. "Wow. If this gets out, there'll be hell to pay. "

"No kidding?" I muttered morosely.

"Jacque, I need you to find out if Ashcroft Chemical has

any current contracts with defense contractors, military research facilities, or foreign governments."

"You think she might be selling the stuff?"

"No... Well..." I shook my head. "I doubt it, but knowing what we've learned, it's possible, I suppose. I think we've only scratched the surface of what Victoria Ashcroft has been up to."

As I drove home that evening, I had a feeling that we were approaching the climax of something much larger and more dangerous than we'd ever imagined. The systematic elimination of witnesses alone, was evidence pointing to environmental terrorism and weapons development, and somewhere out there, Victoria Ashcroft was planning her next move.

10

Shifting Sands

Friday

FRIDAY MORNING BROUGHT A DEVELOPMENT THAT CHANGED everything about how we understood the scope of Victoria Ashcroft's criminal enterprise.

With Amanda still at my father's, I rose early, made myself coffee and toast and was in my office by seven-thirty, going through Jacque's research on political connections, when Kate called my cell phone at just after eight with news that Michael Drake was finally well enough to provide detailed information about his investigation.

"His memory's fully recovered," she said. "And Harry, what he's telling us is crazy, worse than we thought. "

Geez, what now? How the hell can it get any worse? I thought. "How so?" I asked.

"Drake's been investigating Ashcroft and the illegal

dumping operation for over two years. He says Victoria's been systematically eliminating threats for more than a decade."

And there it was; something I'd been dreading. "How many, Kate?"

"Not sure. A lot. Drake thinks the recent murders are just the visible tip of a pattern going back to when her father died."

Geez, so the woman is a serial killer as well, I thought. "Okay, I'm on my way," I said. "Wait for me, will you?"

Thirty minutes later, I was sitting in Drake's hospital room with Kate and Samson, listening to the environmental journalist describe a criminal conspiracy that had been operating with impunity for far longer than we'd imagined.

Drake looked tired but alert, his color much better than when we'd found him on his houseboat. *He couldn't have looked any worse,* I thought, morosely.

He was propped up in bed with several files and a stack of more than twenty photographs on the overbed table: investigative materials retrieved from the safe we'd discovered.

"I've been tracking Victoria's operation for over two years," he rasped, pointing to a folded, but detailed map of Hamilton County that showed dumping locations along the Tennessee River from Williams Island to New Hope. "The illegal disposal goes back more than two decades, but the killing started fifteen years ago, right after Victoria Ashcroft's father's death."

Kate leaned forward, hands clasped together in her lap.

"Fifteen years?" I said. "Can you prove it?"

"No. It's all what you people call circumstantial. But look at these cases," Drake replied, handing me a thick sheaf of newspaper clippings and police reports. "Environmental activists who died in apparent accidents. EPA inspectors who had heart attacks just before major investigations. University researchers whose cars went off mountain roads. All of them had been investigating contamination in the Tennessee River system."

"How many deaths?" I asked.

"At least a dozen that I've been able to document, besides the recent one, probably more. Victoria's been very careful to make them look accidental, space them out over time, use different methods. Until recently, when she started getting sloppy."

Drake picked up a thick file from his side table labeled "Ashcroft Eliminations" and spread several photographs across the table. "The pattern became clear once I started cross-referencing unexplained deaths with environmental investigations. Anyone who got too close to exposing the dumping operation ended up dead."

I studied the photographs and reports. "These all happened in Hamilton County?"

"Hamilton County and the immediate surrounding areas. Victoria's kept her killing spree local, which helped her avoid federal attention for years. But the scope of the environmental damage extends throughout the entire Tennessee River system in this region."

"How did you get into this?" Kate asked.

He coughed, winced, cleared his throat, winced again, then said, "Three years ago, I was working on a story about the water quality of the Tennessee River. I interviewed an EPA inspector named Robert Dun who was investigating contamination patterns around Raccoon Mountain. Two days after our interview, Dun died in a single-car accident on a clear, dry road he'd driven hundreds of times. That triggered something else; a similar death a few months earlier, so I started digging. Dun had mentioned that someone was dumping chemical waste into the river, and that he was close to identifying the source and was planning to recommend federal prosecution."

"Did he say who it was?" I asked.

Drake shook his head. "No. He said he didn't want to release that information until he was sure of his facts."

Suddenly, Samson, who'd been lying quietly beside Kate's chair, rose and walked to the door, his ears turned forward.

"What is it, Sammy?" Kate asked.

"Probably just hospital activity," Drake said, but I noticed he glanced nervously toward the door.

"The night someone tried to kill you," I said. "D'you remember anything at all about your visitor?"

"I've been thinking about that a lot," he replied. "It's still kind of fuzzy, but I remember the person claimed to be interested in collaborating on my environmental investigation. They seemed to know a lot of details about my research that I hadn't published."

"Man or woman?" I asked.

"A woman. I don't remember much about her, but it was definitely a woman. The voice: she was articulate, educated."

"Can you describe her?" Kate asked.

He shrugged, shook his head slowly, then said, "Tallish, I think. Shoulder-length hair. Slim... That's about all I can remember. As I said, it's still fuzzy."

"Could it have been Victoria Ashcroft?" I asked.

"I don't know," he replied. "I've never met her. She refused all my requests for an interview."

Kate's radio crackled with a message from dispatch. "Captain Gazzara, Wildlife is reporting suspicious activity at the old Ashcroft Chemical plant. They have officers on the river and are requesting backup."

"That facility was supposed to be empty," Kate said.

"Maybe someone's finishing up," I replied.

"We have to leave, Mr. Drake," Kate said, "but you'll be safe here. I have an officer posted outside your door, and another in the waiting area.

Drake nodded, then looked at me and said, "Harry, I want you to have this." He handed me a slim file and continued, "This contains a breakdown of everything I've gathered about Victoria's operation over the past two years. If something happens to me—"

"Nothing's going to happen to you," Kate said firmly, interrupting him. "As I just told you, you're safe now. "

"You think?" he asked, sarcastically. "Victoria has resources and connections throughout this county. Money, political influence, people in positions of authority who owe her favors. Anyone who could threaten her operation has either been bought off or eliminated. She's been paying bribes and making campaign contributions for years. Plus, she's got dirt on a lot of people: photographs, recordings, financial records that would destroy careers and send people to prison. If she wants me dead—and she does—she can make it happen, believe me."

"You'll be fine," Kate said. There was nothing else she could say.

"She's right," I said. "We'll check on you later."

―――――

As we drove toward the old Ashcroft Chemical plant, I had a feeling that we were still missing something.

"Kate," I said, "I have no doubt that Drake's right about this being a decades-long operation, and that Victoria Ashcroft is behind it, but don't you think there's something different about these recent murders?"

I turned in my seat to look at her. She was frowning.

"What do you mean?" she asked.

"What if someone else has been doing the killing? Parker and the attack on Drake, yes. But why Jones, Walsh and Murdoch, and the attacks on Muldoon and Marsh? They were all working for her? True, we'd gotten to Muldoon, but she couldn't have known that, could she?"

Kate considered it for a moment as she weaved through the traffic, lights flashing. "Maybe, as you said, there's a leak in the task force. Or maybe the presence of the federal task force spooked her. Who knows?"

"But that would account only for Muldoon," I argued. "Why kill the other three?"

"Okay," she replied. "So maybe someone inside Victoria's operation figured her methods were going to bring down the entire operation and figured self-preservation was better than federal prison."

My phone buzzed with a call from TJ. I answered it on speaker.

"Harry, I think you need to be very careful today," he said. "In light of what's been happening these last couple of weeks, I'm thinking we must be high on the perp's list of targets. Especially you and Kate, and maybe even Tim."

"TJ, this is Kate. What's your assessment of the threat level?"

"High. Very high. I'd recommend you both consider taking backup wherever you're going today."

I thought about Amanda and Jade. The attempted breach

of our security system had already put them at risk, and now TJ was suggesting the danger was escalating.

"TJ, I need you to coordinate with the officers Kate assigned to watch Amanda. She's staying with my father. Maria's there too. Make sure they're up to it and ready for anything. And why don't you have a chat with Maria while you're at it?"

Maria, in case I haven't already mentioned it, is Jade's nanny; well, more than just a nanny. She's ex-ATF, tough as nails, licensed to carry, and an expert shot. I hired her several years ago when... but that's another story.

"Already done, boss," TJ said. "I've also asked Heather to provide additional security for your family."

"Good enough, and thanks, TJ," I said. "Stay in touch." And I hung up.

"That old man is a keeper," Kate said. "You're lucky to have him."

"Don't I know it?" I muttered.

As we approached the old Ashcroft Chemical plant, we could see Tennessee Wildlife boats positioned on the river, their officers watching the facility through binoculars. Kate radioed for their status report.

"There are several vehicles on site and as many as a dozen men and women. It looks like they might be searching the place. "

Kate had already called for backup, so she pulled over on a rise that offered a view of the plant while she waited for them to arrive.

Me? I used the time to study the facility through Kate's binoculars. The old chemical plant was located on a bluff overlooking the river, its aging concrete structures and rusted storage tanks creating the perfect industrial wasteland.

Unfortunately, there were many such structures in and around Chattanooga.

"There's movement on the north side," I said, pointing toward a loading dock where two black SUVs were parked.

"It looks like they're getting ready to leave," Kate said. "Someone's tipped them off, Harry. But this time we're not letting them get away. See?"

I smiled as I watched two SWAT units position themselves at the entrance to the facility.

"Let's get down there, Kate," I said as I watched the black-clad officers stream out of their vehicles into the site.

But before she could put the car into drive, her radio crackled with an update from the SWAT commander. "Captain, we've secured the perimeter, but the facility appears to be empty. The four vehicles we observed have left through the rear access road."

"Damn," Kate muttered. "They're always one step ahead. Someone's going to pay for this, I swear."

There was little else we could do but process the empty facility for the second time in a week.

Kate turned Samson loose and said, "Samson, go seek!" And he streaked off to disappear somewhere inside one of the buildings.

Kate was right, I realized. Whoever was orchestrating these operations must have had access to our communications and planning. They knew when we were coming, what we were looking for, and how to stay ahead of our investigation.

The abandoned laboratory and chemical storage areas told the same story as before: Nothing! Until:

Kate, now ready to leave, called for Samson. He didn't come.

"Sammy, where are you?" she called.

Again, he didn't come. "What the hell?" Kate muttered. "This is not like him. Samson, come!" she shouted.

This time she was rewarded by the sound of barking inside a nearby building.

"Come on," she said, and we, accompanied by two SWAT officers, ran into the building where we found Samson in what once had been a laboratory lying flat on the floor with his nose to a drain cover.

"He's found something," Kate said, snapping on a pair of latex gloves. Then to one of the officers, she said, "Can you remove the cover, please?"

He could, and then stepped back, and Kate, now down on her knees with Samson beside her, his nose almost inside the drain, she reached in and, after a few seconds, discovered a waterproof container.

"Hah," she said, exuberantly waving the container in the air. "You think this is what they were looking for?"

"We won't know until we open it, will we?" I said.

"Right," she said. "So let's take a look, shall we?"

The container wasn't easy to open. It took the SWAT officer and a tactical knife to break the seal, but eventually he got it open and handed it back to Kate. Inside she found several USB drives and a thick notebook containing what appeared to be research notes written in several different hands.

"These notes look like experimental data," she said, her brow and the bridge of her nose wrinkled in concentration.

I studied the notes over her shoulder. The handwriting was scientific, precise, with chemical formulas and what appeared to be test results. But more disturbing were the margin notes that suggested the contaminated water had been monitored for its effects on local communities.

"Kate," I said quietly, "No wonder they were looking for it."

"But if they knew it was here, they'd know where it was," she said. "So why were they looking for it?"

"Maybe they knew it was here but didn't know where it was because its owner was no longer available," I replied.

"No longer avai— Oh, I get it. Dead, you mean?"

I simply shrugged.

She went back to the notes. "So, you mean they were studying the effects on people who drink the water?"

"Or studying how much contamination she could get away with before anyone noticed," I said. "Look at these dosage calculations and time intervals."

We were still studying the notes when my phone rang. It was Amanda, and she sounded worried..

"Harry, something's wrong. The officer Kate assigned to watch us is missing. His radio's not responding, and his car is still outside, but he's nowhere to be found."

I felt my blood pressure spike. "Where are you right now?"

"At August's. Inside the house with Jade and Maria. All the doors are locked, and the security system is active. But Harry, I'm scared. If something's happened to the officer..."

"Stay exactly where you are," I said, already moving toward Kate's SUV. "Lock yourselves in the safe room and don't come out until I get there."

I looked at Kate. She'd heard, and was already calling for backup units to respond to my address while I tried to reach TJ.

His phone rang four times and then went to voicemail. I called again. Same thing.

Kate grabbed my arm. "Harry, come on. We need to go. Now!"

11

***

Undercurrents

Friday, Week 3

FRIDAY AFTERNOON BROUGHT THE BEST NEWS I'D HEARD ALL day, though it came after several terrifying hours. Kate and I had raced to August's house with sirens blaring and backup units following, my mind spinning through worst-case scenarios.

We were still three blocks away when TJ called, cutting through my thoughts.

"Harry, it's okay," he said when I answered. "I've found your missing officer. He'd been dumped in a ditch about two miles away. He was handcuffed and gagged with duct tape, but he'll be fine. The paramedics are with him now."

Geez, that's a relief, but... "What about my family, TJ?"

"Amanda called me fifteen minutes ago," he replied. "They're secure in the safe room, all three of them. Maria's got her shotgun, and she's not taking any chances. Harry, I'm thinking this looks like a message more than an actual threat. The officer was roughed up some, but beyond that he wasn't harmed, and he was left where he'd be found quickly, with his radio and weapon intact. Whoever did this wanted to scare us, not start a body count. You know your dad and Rose are out of town, right?"

"Yeah, I know. They're in Biloxi. He's appearing in a class action."

Kate grabbed the phone from me. "TJ, any witnesses?"

"Negative. No witnesses, nothing left behind. But the timing suggests they knew exactly when to grab him and when we'd discover he was missing. They're telling us they can get to us wherever we are, anytime they want."

"Thanks for the update, TJ," I said, taking back my phone. "We're at the house. I'll call you later."

The house was surrounded by three cruisers, lights flashing, and the reassuring presence of a half-dozen officers securing the perimeter. Amanda's car was still in the garage, and the house showed no signs of forced entry.

My phone rang. It was Amanda. "Harry, where are you?"

"I'm in the driveway. You okay?"

"Yes, but it scared the hell out of me."

"Stay where you are while Kate and her officers clear the house," I said, "Then I'm coming in."

Ten minutes later, after they'd swept every room and confirmed the house was secure, I was finally able to hold my wife and daughter. Jade seemed to think the whole thing was an adventure, while Amanda was clearly shaken, though trying hard not to show it.

"Joe, the officer, was sitting on the bench outside the front door and then he just… vanished," Amanda said quietly while

Jade played with Samson in the living room. "One minute he was there. The next he was gone. Maria went to look for him, then came back a minute later, and we locked ourselves in the safe room. Harry, why didn't you answer your phone? I called and called. I even called Kate."

"I called you, too," I said. "They must have been jamming the signal. Well, it's over now and you're all safe. That's all that matters."

"What about Joe?" she asked.

"TJ called. Joe's okay, except for his wounded pride, maybe."

"But why take him at all?" Kate asked. "Why not just eliminate the threat?"

"Because, as TJ said, they wanted to send a message," I replied.

"Which means they're not done with us yet," Amanda said quietly.

"No," I agreed. "But it also means they're not about to escalate to killing law enforcement officers. Not yet, anyway."

"Well, that's something," she replied. "What about the investigation? Any developments over the weekend?"

"Actually, yes. Tim's been working on the USB drives and research notes we found at the chemical plant. It seems we underestimated the scope of Victoria's operation."

"How so?" she asked.

It was then that I realized what she was doing. "Oh no," I said. "Everything I said or say is off the record. One leak in this investigation is more than enough."

She smiled at me and said, "Now, Harry, as if I would?"

"Oh, you would," I replied. "You'll just have to wait before you... do your thing."

"If you say so," she replied. "So, are you going to tell me how you underestimated Victoria?"

It was at that moment my phone rang and saved me. It was Tim. "Harry, is Amanda okay? 'Cause if she is, you and Kate should probably get down here. There's been another development."

"Oh, geez," I thought. *Not more bad news.* "What is it this time, Tim?"

There was a moment of silence, then Tim said, "Agent Mornay says to tell you that you and Kate are needed here."

"Damn!" I muttered, then said, "Okay, I'm on my way." I hung up and then turned again to Amanda and said, "I don't think you'll hear from them again. You'll be okay?" It was a question, not a statement.

She nodded. "Of course."

"TJ will be here in a few minutes," I said, "and I'll have Kate leave some of her officers. I'll be back as soon as I can."

Five minutes later, Kate and I were on our way down the mountain and heading for the police department on Amnicola Highway. Twenty minutes after that, we walked into the conference room and sat down at the table. Samson took up his usual position at Kate's feet.

"So tell me," I said, "what's so damn urgent I had to leave my family after they've just been scared half to death?"

Mornay and Collins turned their heads to look at Tim.

He gave me a wry smile, raised his shoulders in a half shrug, then said, "I've been analyzing the data on the USB drives. There's over three years of detailed financial records." Tim paused for a second, staring at his screen, then adjusted his glasses and continued, "She's been bringing in hazardous materials from all over the country and disposing of it illegally in the Tennessee River."

I frowned. It wasn't something I didn't already know, and I said so. "That doesn't surprise me, and it shouldn't surprise any of you, either. It would have been a natural progression. So I still can't understand why you couldn't have waited until tomorrow to tell me."

"You're part of the investigation, that's why," Johnston snapped.

"With respect, Chief," I replied. "I'm an unpaid consultant, not a cop. And you've had exclusive access to Tim for four days now. D'you have any idea what that would cost if you had to pay for it?" I saw Tim grin out of the corner of my eye.

"You want out, Harry?" he asked testily.

"You know the answer to that," I replied. "It's no. I'm here because of Kate, but don't expect me to jump on the shovel every time one of these two shouts shit."

"OKAY! That's enough," Kate shouted. "This is not a pissing contest. Let's get back to what matters. Tim, what else d'you have for us?"

I glanced at Johnston. He looked shocked. His eyes were narrowed almost to slits. He looked about as angry as I'd ever seen him, but he said nothing. I looked at Kate. Her face was red, but otherwise she looked at ease. Sammy, however, was on his feet. She put her hand down, patted his head, and he sat down again.

"Go on, Tim," I said.

He stuck out his bottom lip, thought for a moment, then said, "What she's doing is... Well, I already told you. Okay, so companies from all around the country have been paying Victoria to 'properly dispose' of their hazardous waste. Instead, she's been dumping it all right here in the Tennessee River and pocketing millions in disposal fees."

"Which explains why she's been so desperate to eliminate

threats," I said. "She's protecting a multi-million-dollar criminal enterprise."

Agent Collins leaned forward. "How much money are we talking about, Tim?"

"Over ninety million dollars in disposal fees collected in the past three years alone," Tim replied, consulting his notes. "And that's just what I can document. The operation's probably been running for much longer."

The last estimate had been fifty million; now we were at almost double that.

Chief Johnston whistled. "Ninety million? No wonder she's been killing people to protect it."

Agent Mornay spread out shipping manifests across the table. "These documents show regular deliveries from chemical companies in twenty-seven states, pharmaceutical manufacturers, even some defense contractors. All paying premium rates."

"And it's all been dumped into the Tennessee River system," Collins said.

Tim's computer chimed with an incoming alert. He frowned at the screen, typed rapidly for a couple of seconds, then looked up at me with obvious concern.

"We've got a problem," he said. "Someone's up to something."

"Up to what?" Collins asked.

But before Tim could answer, Kate's radio crackled with a message from dispatch: "Captain Gazzara, we have reports of explosions at two locations: a boat at the Chickamauga marina and the UTC Environmental Sciences building. The fire department is responding to both scenes."

"They're destroying evidence," I said.

"Whatever," Kate said, looking at the chief. "I'll keep you informed," she said as she rose to her feet.

Johnston nodded.

Kate looked at me. "You coming?" she asked, already moving toward the door with Samson at her side.

I stood, looked at the chief and winked. He didn't respond, nor did I expect him to, but I had a feeling this would be the last time he would approve my participation. But you know what? I didn't give a damn. It would be his loss, not mine, and he sure as hell hadn't been shy about asking me to find his daughter when she went missing all those years ago. But that is also another story.

———

As we raced toward the UTC campus with sirens blaring, I realized the timing was too perfect to be coincidental, and I was more sure than ever that we had a traitor inside the task force.

The environmental sciences building was engulfed in flames when we arrived. Fire department units were already on scene, but the intensity of the blaze suggested accelerants had been used throughout the structure.

"There's no way this is accidental," Kate said, watching the flames consume the building that had housed Dr. Parker's research.

Fire Chief McNally approached. He was sweating despite the chilly October day. "How you doin', Kate?" he asked and then, without waiting for her to answer, said, "We're not going to be able to save the building."

"Arson?" she asked, staring at the burning building.

"We won't know that for sure for days," he replied, "but judging by the intensity, it would be my guess."

A moment later my phone buzzed with a call from TJ. "Harry, I'm at the marina," he said. "Someone tried to torch Drake's houseboat about an hour ago."

Kate moved closer so she could hear. "How bad is the damage, TJ?"

"Could have been worse," he replied. "And don't worry, Harry. There are four officers at your father's home. Anyway, a passing fisherman spotted the smoke and called 911 before it really got going. The fire department managed to save the boat, but the main cabin's a mess. Good job Drake's still in the hospital. But here's the thing: whoever did this was looking for something. They tore the place apart before they torched it. Drawers pulled out, cushions slashed, even the floorboards pried up in places."

"There was nothing to find," Kate said. "We already recovered his files from the safe."

"That's what I'm thinking too," TJ replied. "Maybe they didn't know about the safe, or maybe they were looking for something else. Either way, they wanted to make sure nothing was left behind. I hope to hell Drake had insurance."

"TJ, you said an hour ago, right?" I asked.

"Yup. An hour."

"That's around the same time as the UTC explosion," I said to Kate.

"Within about thirty minutes, or so, yes," she replied. "Someone's getting desperate."

By then, Agent Mornay had joined us, and she was looking grim.

"Harry, Kate," she said by way of greeting. "This looks bad."

"It is bad," I said. "Our killer has to be someone who knew exactly what evidence we'd collected and where it was stored."

"Any thoughts about who it might be?" she asked.

"Could be anyone," I replied. "Crime scene people, investigators—you and Collins have enough of them with you to start an entirely new department." I looked at her, narrowed my eyes and said, "even you or Collins."

At that she almost choked. Me? I grinned at her, but somehow she didn't find it funny.

As afternoon turned toward evening, we regrouped at the police department to assess what remained of our investigation. Dr. Sally's physical evidence was gone, most of the financial records had been stored at locations that were now smoking ruins. We could only hope she'd backed everything up, but at least our key witnesses were still alive and protected.

"We need to contact Dr. Howard immediately," Kate said, grabbing her phone. "If she still has those backup files, she's our only remaining source of evidence. And if someone's destroying everything connected to Parker's research..."

"She's a target," I finished. "We need to get her into protective custody."

Kate was already dialing Sally's number. It rang four times before going to voicemail.

"Dr. Howard, this is Captain Gazzara. Please call me immediately. It's urgent."

She tried the university number next. After being transferred twice, she reached someone in the Marine Biology department.

"Dr. Howard left about an hour ago," the department secretary said. "She seemed upset about something and said she needed to go home to check on her security system."

Kate and I exchanged worried glances. "Did she say why?" Kate asked.

"Something about her house alarm going off. She got a call from the security company."

"We're going to her house," Kate said, already heading for the door with Samson. "Now."

Fifteen minutes later, we were standing outside Dr. Sally Howard's modest home in East Brainerd. Her car was in the driveway, the front door was slightly ajar, and there were no lights on inside despite the approaching darkness.

"This doesn't feel right," I said, drawing my weapon.

Kate called for backup while I approached the front door. "Dr. Howard? Chattanooga Police."

No response.

We found Sally in her home office, slumped over her desk. She was unconscious but breathing, a small puncture wound visible behind her left ear.

"Same injection site as the others," Kate said, checking her pulse. "But she's alive."

Paramedics arrived within minutes and an hour later the hospital confirmed that Sally had been injected with a sedative, not the lethal tetrodotoxin used on the murder victims.

"Why sedate her instead of killing her?" Kate asked as we examined Sally's ransacked office.

"Because they needed something from her first," I replied, pointing to the empty filing cabinets and overturned desk drawers. "They were looking for those backup files."

Kate's phone rang. It was the hospital.

"Dr. Howard is conscious and asking for you," the nurse said. "She says it's urgent."

Twenty minutes later, we were sitting beside Sally's hospital bed. She was groggy but alert, and clearly frightened.

"They took everything," she said weakly. "All of Jennifer's backup files, my research notes, even my computer hard drives."

"Sally," Kate said, "the people who attacked you. Can you describe what happened?"

Sally's face went pale as she recalled the attack. "Two men grabbed me as soon as I walked through my front door. They were waiting inside. Big guys. They blindfolded me before I could get a good look at them."

"Then what happened?" I asked.

"They tied me to my chair in my office and searched the house for maybe twenty minutes. Then someone else arrived, a woman. I heard her giving orders to the men, telling them where to look."

Kate leaned forward. "Could you see this woman?"

"No, the blindfold was tight. But I knew who it was. I could hear her voice clearly." Sally's voice dropped to a whisper. "It was Victoria Ashcroft."

Now that was something! "Are you certain?" I asked, cutting Kate off before she could speak.

"Absolutely. I've met her many times. I also met her at the aquarium the night Jennifer was killed. That voice is unmistakable: educated, authoritative, with just a hint of a Southern accent. It was definitely Victoria."

"Then what happened?" Kate asked.

"She asked me about Jennifer's backup files. She knew exactly what to ask for: the storage facility location, the access codes, even the false name Jennifer used to rent the unit." Sally started crying again. "She said if I didn't cooperate, they'd kill me."

"How did she know about the backup files?" I asked.

"That's what terrified me. Victoria knew details that only

Jennifer and I discussed. She knew about the Neptune access code, the off-site storage, even the specific research Jennifer was planning to share with the federal investigators."

Kate and I exchanged glances. This confirmed that Victoria had been monitoring Parker's activities closely, probably through Dr. Jones.

"Sally," Kate said gently, "what happened after you gave them the information?"

"Victoria told the men to inject me with something. She said it would just put me to sleep, that they didn't want to kill me." Sally shuddered. "I screamed. I didn't believe her. The last thing I remember is Victoria saying they needed to get to the storage unit before you figured out what was missing."

Kate and I stepped outside Sally's room to talk privately.

"So Victoria's directly involved in the evidence destruction," Kate said grimly

"And if what Professor Howard says is true, and I can't see why it wouldn't be, she has professional help," I added. "Two men who knew how to execute a home invasion without leaving witnesses or evidence."

"The question is how Victoria knew about the backup files in the first place," Kate said. "Sally said she and Jennifer were the only ones who knew about the storage unit."

"Unless Jennifer told someone else," I replied. "Or unless Victoria was monitoring their communications. I think that's probably the most likely answer, but why did she wait so long to make her move?"

But only Victoria herself could answer that question. Then again, it had only been two weeks since Jennifer Parker's death. Not so long at all, really.

"Harry," Kate said quietly, "if Victoria's willing to personally oversee the elimination of evidence, what do you think she'll do when she realizes we're getting close to arresting her?"

"For what?" I asked. "All we have is Sally Howard's word that it was Victoria that attacked her. She was blindfolded. Any kind of lawyer would be quick to point out that she could be wrong about recognizing the voice, and he'd be right. And, Victoria has an ironclad alibi for Jennifer Parker's murder."

———

BY SIX THAT MONDAY EVENING, we were once again gathered in the PD conference room going over the details of the day's events.

"Victoria seems to be eliminating her entire support network," Agent Collins said, reviewing the timeline of deaths and attacks. "Jones, Walsh, Murdoch, the attempts on Muldoon and Marsh—they're all connected to the illegal dumping operation."

"So why would she eliminate her own people? They were all still useful to her... Well, at least as far as she knew. Muldoon, as we know, had turned."

"Maybe she's panicking," Mornay suggested. "Maybe the federal investigation spooked her and she thinks it's safer to eliminate everyone who could testify against her rather than trust them to stay quiet."

"That would make sense, " I said. "They had inside knowledge of the dumping operation. And Jones was feeding Victoria information. Walsh was providing political protection. The chain is, as they say, only as strong as its weakest link, and we'd already broken one link."

"Yes, but there's something that bothers me about the precision of these attacks," Kate said, "and I'm including

Drake, the boat, Sally Howard and the UTC Environmental Studies Department. They're almost too perfect."

Tim looked up from his computer in the corner. "Whoever it is has access to some pretty serious stuff. Tetrodotoxin isn't something you can just buy online. It requires scientific knowledge to extract and prepare."

"And they'd need to know who was involved in Victoria's operation," I added. "Someone with inside access to information about the conspiracy."

Agent Collins leaned back in his chair. "So, we're looking for someone with scientific training who knew about the illegal dumping and had personal reasons to eliminate everyone involved. That's not asking much, is it?" he asked sarcastically.

"How about revenge?" Kate asked thoughtfully. "That's always a good motive."

Chief Johnston had been listening quietly. "Kate, are you suggesting someone's been conducting a revenge campaign against Victoria's operation?"

"Nah, not really," she replied. "Just throwing stuff against the wall to see if any of it sticks."

Tim's computer chimed with an alert. "I've been analyzing the financial records: the payments to Jones, Walsh, and the boat operators all came from the same shell company account."

"Which means?" Kate asked, sounding about as tired and fed up as I was.

"It means whoever had access to that account would know exactly who was being paid and for what. They'd have a complete list of everyone involved in the conspiracy."

I sat up in my seat. "Damn!" I said. "Why didn't I think of that? Tim, who all had access to those account records?"

He grinned. "Anyone with administrative access to the shell companies. That could include Victoria herself, her lawyer, maybe a trusted executive or accountant."

"We need to identify everyone with access to Victoria's financial information and cross-reference them with people who have marine biology expertise," Collins said, stating the obvious.

"And people who had personal connections to Dr. Parker," Kate added.

"There's something else," Mornay said. "You've been intimating for a week now that we have a leak within the task force. What are we going to do about that?"

"It has to be an inside person," Chief Johnston said grimly.

"Or someone who's been watching our investigation closely," I replied. "Someone with legitimate reason to monitor our progress."

Kate's phone buzzed with a message from the hospital. Sally Howard was being discharged and was requesting additional police protection.

Me? I figured it was a good time to go home to my family.

12

Watershed

Wednesday Week 4

WEDNESDAY MORNING FOUND ME STARING AT THE CEILING AT five AM, my mind refusing to shut down despite my body's desperate need for rest. The previous night had been another exercise in futility, tossing and turning while my brain replayed every detail of Victoria Ashcroft's systematic destruction of evidence and Sally Howard's terrifying account of her attack.

By six-thirty, I gave up on sleep and made my way to the kitchen, where I made coffee. Amanda, who, after insisting loudly, was now back home with Jade, followed a few moments later wearing one of my old t-shirts and pajama pants, her strawberry blonde hair pulled back in a messy ponytail; she looked as tired as I felt.

"You had a rough night again," she stated as she poured and then handed me a steaming mug. "You kept me awake half the night, too."

"Sorry. It's getting to be a habit," I replied, settling into my usual chair at the breakfast table. "My brain won't turn off. Every time I close my eyes, I see that burning building at UTC, or think about Sally Howard tied to a chair while Victoria Ashcroft interrogates her."

Amanda poured herself coffee and sat down across from me. "Come on, Harry," she said after taking a sip of her coffee. "You've identified who attacked Sally Howard and destroyed the evidence. That's progress."

"Yes, Victoria Ashcroft, but we can't prove any of it," I said, frustrated. "But here's the thing: the systematic elimination of her network makes little sense if she's doing it. Why would she kill the people who were loyal to her? Jones was feeding her information. Walsh was providing political protection. God only knows what Murdoch was into. The boat operators were carrying out her dumping operations. I can't get my head around it."

Amanda considered this while sipping her coffee. "You're right," she said eventually. "It makes no sense unless she's decided to eliminate everyone who could testify against her."

"Yeah, that's what Mornay said," I replied. "Or maybe it's someone else with reasons of their own who's killing off her people."

Jade appeared in the doorway, rubbing her eyes and dragging her favorite stuffed animal; a well-worn teddy bear named Mr. Buttons. As I lifted her up onto her chair, I couldn't help but notice, for at least the thousandth time, that she had Amanda's green eyes. The little monster also had my stubborn streak, along with an uncanny ability to sense when the adults around her were worried.

"Daddy, why are you up so early?" she asked.

"Just couldn't sleep, princess," I said, kissing the top of her head. "How about some pancakes for breakfast?"

"With chocolate chips?" she asked hopefully.

"If that's what you want."

As I made pancakes and Amanda helped Jade get ready for school, I thought back over the past three weeks, about the pattern of the attacks and murders, how each victim had posed a different type of threat to Victoria's operation, or not, and the more I thought about it, the more frustrated I became. In the end, I gave it up, deciding to spend what little time I had before I had to leave with my two girls.

The kitchen felt warm and normal, a stark contrast to the violence that had been consuming my thoughts. Jade chattered happily about her upcoming school play while Amanda braided her hair, and for a moment I tried to push away the images of crime scenes and injection sites that had been haunting my sleep.

"Daddy, are you listening?" Jade asked, tugging on my shirt.

"Sorry, princess. Tell me again about your costume."

"I'm going to be a tree in the forest scene, and Mrs. Peterson says I get to wear brown and green and have leaves in my hair," she said excitedly. "Will you come and watch?"

"I wouldn't miss it," I said, realizing how much I needed these moments of normalcy to balance the darkness of the investigation.

I set a plate of chocolate chip pancakes in front of Jade, who immediately began arranging them in a pattern before eating

My phone buzzed with a call from Kate. I answered it while continuing to cook.

"Harry, it's me," she said, stating the obvious. "We've got another body. This time it's Victoria's lawyer. In his office downtown."

I heaved a sigh, shook my head, and said, "When?"

"The building security guard found him around midnight. He's been dead for several hours, according to the preliminary assessment."

"I'll be there quick as I can," I said, already turning off the stove.

Amanda looked at me with concern. "Another murder?"

"Yep. This time it's Victoria's lawyer."

She didn't answer, but I could see she was upset. Me? I also said nothing. If you think about it, there was really nothing I *could* say.

So, after I finished dressing, ensured Amanda and Jade were secure with their protection detail, I kissed them both and drove downtown to the law offices of Mitchell, Crane & Associates.

The building was one of those gleaming glass towers that had sprung up in Chattanooga's revitalized downtown core, housing the kind of high-end legal practice that specialized in corporate defense and damage control.

Kate was waiting for me in the lobby with Samson, along with Agent Collins and Agent Mornay. The building had been locked down, and crime scene tape blocked access to the upper floors.

"Morning, all," I said. "What do we know?"

"The victim is Robert Crane, senior partner, fifty-eight years old," Kate replied, consulting her notes. "According to building security, he was working late on what he called an urgent client matter."

"Victoria Ashcroft?" I asked.

"That's what we're assuming. Crane's been Victoria's primary legal counsel for over a decade. He handled the corporate structuring for her shell companies and managed her political donations."

Collins led us to the elevator. "The security guard found him slumped over his desk around midnight," he said. "The door was locked from the inside with no signs of forced entry, and nothing disturbed except for some missing files."

"Missing files about what?" I asked. "And how do we know they're missing?"

"According to his secretary," Collins replied, "Crane had been working on what he called 'crisis management documents' for Ashcroft Chemical. Legal strategies for dealing with federal environmental investigations, and she can't find the file."

"Got it," I said. "So, now, on top of everything else, we have a locked door mystery to contend with. How very frickin' ironic!"

We rode the elevator the rest of the way to the fifteenth floor in silence. Robert Crane's office was a monument to legal success: floor-to-ceiling windows overlooking the downtown business district, expensive furniture, walls lined with law books and framed certificates. And in the center of it all, a very dead lawyer.

Dr. Hensley was completing her examination when we arrived. She looked up from her clipboard as we entered. "More of the same, I'm afraid," she said. "There's an injection site behind the left ear, so I'm assuming tetrodotoxin poisoning causing paralysis before death. It will have to be confirmed, of course, as will my estimate of the time of death: between nine and ten last night."

Kate and I exchanged glances. She turned to Mornay and said, "Any idea how the killer gained access?"

"The building security shows someone exiting the elevator on the fifteenth floor at nine-seventeen," Mornay replied. "But whoever it was, was wearing a hoodie, so there's no clear view of the person's face."

"Male or female?" I asked, as I gave the door lock a cursory look.

"Difficult to tell," Mornay said. "Average height, dark clothing, appeared to know exactly where they were going."

"That figures," I said, then, turning away from the door, "There's no mystery here. Crane must have let his killer in. They simply locked the door from inside before leaving and pulled it closed behind them. It's a standard office lock. Opens with a key card."

I examined Crane's desk while the others discussed security footage. According to his secretary, not only were several file folders missing, so was his laptop computer, all of which contained confidential documents related to Ashcroft Chemical. But the killer *had* left behind an appointment calendar that showed meetings scheduled throughout the week with various clients, including a notation for the previous evening that simply read "A.C. - Crisis Management."

The office itself told a story of interrupted work. Papers were spread across the desk in a way that suggested Crane had been actively working when he was attacked. A half-empty coffee cup to his right, still contained what, after a quick sniff, appeared to be the remnants of an expensive blend. His jacket hung neatly on the back of his chair, and his briefcase sat open beside the desk, files still visible inside.

I snapped on a pair of latex gloves and followed Samson around the office—his nose twitching as he examined every corner of the room—noting the details that might provide clues about Crane's final hours. The law books on his shelves were meticulously organized, with several volumes pulled out and left open on the credenza to sections dealing with environmental law and corporate liability. A yellow legal pad on his desk was covered with handwritten notes in what appeared to be preparation for legal arguments: references to federal environmental statutes, precedential cases, and what looked like defensive strategies for someone facing serious criminal charges.

"Kate," I said, studying the legal pad more carefully, "look at these notes. I'm no lawyer, but it looks like Crane was preparing a defense strategy for someone facing environmental terrorism charges."

She joined me at the desk, reading over my shoulder. "Looks like it," she said then stepped away.

"And look at this," I pointed to a series of dollar amounts written in the margin. "These look like settlement figures or potential fines. We're talking about hundreds of millions of dollars in potential liability."

She stared at the notes, frowning, then looked at me and said, "No wonder she's panicking."

"And look at this," I said, pulling the appointment book closer. "Crane was expecting someone last night."

She studied the calendar entry. "A.C. could mean anything," she said. "Ashcroft Chemical. Or it could someone else entirely."

"The timing fits. If Crane was meeting with Victoria or someone representing her interests at around eight-thirty, and he died between nine and ten..."

"The killer could have been Victoria herself, or... almost anyone," Kate finished.

"But here's what bothers me," I said, pointing to the legal pad again. "These defense strategies aren't just for environmental crimes. Look at this section here. He was researching defenses for accessory to murder charges. I don't think Crane was working on crisis management for Victoria. I think he was doing it for himself. I think he knew what Victoria was doing and was afraid he was going to get hauled in as an accessory. And if he was, and if she knew about it, then that's motive for killing him, right?"

Kate studied the notes more carefully. "I dunno, Harry. What you're saying makes sense, but..." She trailed off. Obviously, she had doubts, and at that point so did I. It was after all just a theory, but still...

"As always," she muttered, "too many questions and not enough answers."

I turned away from the desk to find Collins talking to the building security supervisor. "Access to this floor," the woman was saying, "requires either a key card or someone buzzing you up from the lobby. At that time of night, Mr. Crane would have had to have buzzed his visitor up."

Collins thanked her and then turned to me and said, "You heard that, I assume. Crane's secretary confirmed it. She says he often worked late and would buzz his clients up."

By then, Dr. Hensley had packed up her equipment. "Captain Gazzara," she said, "I'll have the full autopsy results by tomorrow morning, but the preliminary findings are consistent with the previous victims. I assume that's enough for you to work with, for now at least."

As Kate thanked the medical examiner and she prepared to leave, I studied her carefully. She'd been present at every crime scene, had access to all our forensic evidence, and was in a perfect position to provide information to anyone interested in staying ahead of our investigation.

"Kate," I said quietly, "have you noticed that Dr. Hensley is always precise about the time of death?"

She shook her head, wrinkled her brow, and said, "No. What do you mean?"

"I mean, she seems unusually confident. Between nine and ten. That's narrow. Doc would have given us a couple of hours, at best. "

Kate considered this. "You think she's being deliberately specific?"

I sighed, shook my head, then said, "I don't know what I think, Kate. I'm just thrashing around trying to find something to cling onto. But think about it, someone with her expertise could easily manipulate time of death estimates to protect or implicate people."

"Geez, Harry, that's one hell of a stretch, even for you. She works for the hospital, for Pete's sake."

"Yeah, I know," I said and sighed again.

We spent the rest of the morning processing Crane's office and interviewing the building's security staff. The pattern was becoming depressingly familiar: a professional execution, minimal evidence, and the elimination of someone who could provide damning testimony about Victoria's criminal enterprise.

The security interviews revealed additional details that painted a picture of careful planning. The building's head of security, a retired police sergeant named Stacy Williams, provided us with a timeline that should have shown unusual activity in the days leading up to Crane's murder, only there wasn't any.

"Harry," Kate said. She'd been searching Crane's desk drawers. "Look at this." She held up what looked like a small, leather-bound notebook. "I found this in the bottom drawer. It looks like Crane was documenting payments to various officials and contractors. These look like bribes and payoffs going back years."

She handed it to me. It was a handwritten ledger. The entries showed regular payments to city council members, county commissioners, EPA inspectors, and even some law enforcement officials. The amounts were substantial: tens of thousands of dollars spread across dozens of recipients over many years.

"Victoria's been buying protection throughout Hamilton County," I said. "No wonder the political pressure to shut down our investigation has been so intense."

But as we prepared to leave the law firm, Agent Mornay received a call that added yet another disturbing element to our investigation.

"That was FBI financial crimes division," she said after hanging up. "They've been tracking electronic transactions related to the shell companies in Victoria's operation. There was a massive transfer of funds yesterday afternoon: twenty million dollars was moved to several offshore accounts."

"Someone's liquidating assets," Kate said.

"Or someone's preparing to disappear," I replied. "If Victoria realizes her entire network is being eliminated, she might be planning to run."

"Or she might be planning something else," Agent Collins suggested. "Someone who's been willing to commit murder to protect a criminal enterprise isn't likely to just give up and flee."

I had to agree with that. And I had a deep-seated feeling in my gut that Agent Collins was right and that there were more deaths to come. And as we drove back to the police department, I couldn't shake the feeling that we were approaching some kind of climax. The systematic elimination of Victoria's associates, the massive transfer of funds, the escalating violence: it all pointed to some sort of final confrontation.

"Kate," I said, "what if Victoria's not the one liquidating assets? What if it's someone else?"

"You mean the person who's been eliminating her network is positioning themselves to take control of the company?"

I smiled at that. "I hadn't thought of that," I replied. "It would be the ultimate in corporate takeovers, wouldn't it?"

"Wouldn't it just?" she replied.

"Then again, they might be planning to destroy the entire operation and everyone connected to it," I said.

Kate considered this as we stopped at a red light. "Any of those would explain the financial transfers: Victoria's about to do a runner; a corporate takeover; someone wants to destroy her operation completely. Geez, it's... I dunno what it is, other than a frickin' mess."

"But the last two would take someone with intimate knowledge of her business operations," I said. "Someone who knew account numbers, access codes, the locations of offshore holdings, the whole schmeer."

My phone buzzed with a text from TJ: "Something's going on at the old Ashcroft Chemical plant. It looks like they're making preparations for something."

I showed the message to Kate. "TJ's been monitoring the chemical plant since yesterday."

"Maybe someone's making their move," Kate said.

I called TJ back. "TJ, is this something we need to be concerned about right now?"

"Negative, Harry," he replied. "Just a bunch of people moving around, but they're staying inside the perimeter. Looks like security, or preparation, not immediate action."

"All right, TJ. Keep your eyes open and let me know if the situation changes."

"Will do, boss," he replied, and I hung up.

13

Blood in the Water

Thursday

THURSDAY MORNING BROUGHT NEWS THAT CONFIRMED OUR worst fears about Victoria Ashcroft's increasing desperation. I was barely awake when Kate called just before six.

"What the hell, Kate?" I said, struggling to sit up in bed. "D'you know what time it is?"

"Yes, it's six o'clock. Get your lazy ass up. There's been a break in at the Ashcroft Chemical headquarters in the downtown office building on Broad Street. And we have another body, Randolf Webb, Ashcroft Chemical's chief operating officer."

I swung my legs off the bed. "When?"

"Harry?" Amanda said, sleepily. "What on earth?"

I put a finger to my lips as I listened to Kate. Amanda simply rolled over and pretended to go back to sleep.

"Security found him around midnight," Kate said. "When they responded to the break-in alarm. He'd been dead for several hours. Harry, the chief's going to be all over this. It's the fifth murder in less than a week. Add Dr. Parker to the list; the total's six."

"Victoria's entire support network must be all but gone," I said, running a hand through my hair, heading for the bathroom. "Jones, Walsh, Murdoch, Crane, now Webb. She must be in full panic mode by now."

"There's more," Kate continued. "The corporate offices were ransacked. Financial records, computer hard drives, backup servers; everything's been destroyed or stolen. I just got the call. I'll be there in an hour. Can you meet me there? We need to process the scene, and Agent Collins is having a tizzy."

"I bet he is," I said. "Yeah, give me an hour."

After a quick shower, two cups of black coffee and a slice of toast, and my reassuring Amanda that I'd be careful, I was in my car heading down the mountain on Scenic Highway. By then it was after seven, and the city was waking. But my mind, now wide awake, was racing through the implications of Webb's murder and what we thought was our understanding of the killer's ultimate objectives. I no longer believed it was Victoria Ashcroft. There was no way she was going to eliminate her network, so who the hell was eliminating it?

It was the fundamental question that was holding it all together, but my gut was telling me we were missing something crucial about the killer's identity and motivation. Each murder had been executed with the same clinical precision—yes, Webb's was, too, as I was soon to find out—which suggested someone with extensive knowledge of both

Ashcroft's criminal operation and the task force's law enforcement procedures.

I parked behind the yellow tapes, exited the car, nodded to Kate, who was waiting on the steps, and stared up at the high-rise. The Ashcroft Chemical corporate headquarters occupied three floors of a modern office building on Broad Street, just a few blocks from the Tennessee River. *How convenient,* I thought.

The building's glass facade reflected the early morning light, giving no hint of the violence that had occurred inside just hours earlier.

The building was surrounded on three sides by police vehicles, federal agents, and crime scene technicians. The scene had the controlled chaos that characterizes a major criminal investigation: uniformed officers maintaining perimeter security, detectives interviewing witnesses, and federal agents coordinating with local authorities.

Kate, as I said, was waiting for me on the steps with Samson.

"Geez," she said as I ran up the three steps. "Thank God. They're already here, inside, in the lobby: Agents Collins and Mornay."

"They beat you to it, huh?" I said with a half-smile.

She looked tired, like she'd been up most of the night, but she still managed to give me one of those looks, but there was also a grim determination in her expression that told me she wasn't about to take any crap; not even from me.

"Come on, let's do this," she said and turned and walked through the glass doors into the lobby, where we were met by Collins and Mornay.

"Morning," I said. "I take it you've been up there. What's the scene look like?"

"Someone knew what they were doing," Collins replied, and I got the impression he was harboring a grudging admiration for the killer's efficiency. "Whoever did this knew exactly what they were looking for and how to find it," he continued. "They accessed secured areas, bypassed multiple security systems, and eliminated specific types of evidence while leaving other materials untouched."

"Any witnesses?" I asked.

"The building security guard was making his rounds when the alarm was triggered," Mornay said. "He saw someone leaving through the rear emergency exit, but the lighting was poor and he couldn't provide a detailed description. But here's the thing: whoever it was, triggered the alarm on purpose. They wanted us to know."

"Male or female?" Kate asked.

"Couldn't tell. Average height, dark clothing, in a hurry. They got in and got out."

We rode the elevator to the executive floor in silence. The corporate offices of Ashcroft Chemical were a wonderland that reflected the company's apparent success: expensive furniture, original artwork, floor-to-ceiling windows. But the signs of destruction were strewn everywhere.

File cabinets had been emptied; the contents dumped on the floor. Computer workstations were flashing with signs that said, 'Deletion Complete.' And papers were scattered across the floor like a carpet.

It appeared that Randolf Webb's corner office had been the epicenter of the break-in. His computer equipment was missing, his desk drawers cleaned out, and the contents scattered across the floor. Webb himself was slumped in his chair behind an antique mahogany desk that must have cost a small fortune.

"It's a carbon copy," I said as I looked around. "Webb must have known and trusted his killer."

"I agree," Dr. Hensley said as she continued wrapping up her examination. She looked up at me and laid her clipboard down on the desk. She too looked tired, and I couldn't help but notice a slight tremor in her hands.

"You're right," she said and sat down on the edge of the desk. "There's an injection site behind the left ear. I can't say for sure that it's tetrodotoxin poisoning until I have the tox results, but that would be my guess. Time of death somewhere between eight and nine last night."

Kate took notes while Samson and I examined the office. "Any idea how the killer gained access to the building?" she asked.

"The building security system shows someone using Webb's access card around 7:30 PM," Mornay replied. "It was either someone Webb knew and trusted, or someone who had somehow obtained his security credentials."

"Or cloned them," I muttered.

"Or someone who'd taken his card by force," Kate suggested, studying the scattered papers on Webb's desk.

I joined her, and among the debris, I found fragments of documents. Shipping manifests for hazardous waste deliveries, financial records showing payments to boat operators, correspondence with EPA officials, and a whole lot more.

"Kate," I said, "Webb would have known every detail of Victoria's operation—timing, locations, personnel, financial arrangements. He must have been in it up to his neck."

"Which would have made him incredibly valuable," she said.

"And incredibly dangerous to Victoria herself," I added. "If Webb had been arrested and decided to cooperate with the federal authorities, he could have provided enough testimony to convict everyone involved in the conspiracy, including Victoria. Maybe that's her motive for the murders."

Collins was reviewing security footage on a laptop. "There's something interesting about the timeline here. The break-in alarm was triggered at eleven-forty-seven last night, but according to Dr. Hensley's examination, Webb was already dead by as much as two hours by then."

"Which means the killer spent several hours searching the offices after murdering Webb," Kate said.

"I think they were looking for something specific, which, by the look of the mess, they didn't find," I said, rubbing my chin. "I dunno; maybe they did find it. But whatever it was, it was something important enough to risk staying in the building for hours after committing murder."

I continued to examine Webb's office, noting details I thought might provide insights into the killer's methods and objectives, while Collins continued to examine the building's security systems.

"The killer also disabled specific surveillance cameras while leaving the others operational," Collins said, almost conversationally. "They created blind spots that allowed movement through the building without being recorded, but they left cameras active in areas where they weren't operating."

"This wasn't a crime of opportunity," Kate said. "It was a carefully orchestrated operation. More than one person, d'you think?" she asked, looking at me.

"Could be," I replied, thoughtfully staring at Samson, who was lying down under one of the big windows. "I don't think we're going to find anything significant, Kate. Look at Sammy. He looks bored to death."

She heaved a huge sigh, shook her head, her ponytail swishing, then said, "I don't know, Harry. Maybe you're right. Let's leave it to Willis and his team. You up for some breakfast?"

I was, but it didn't happen. Just as we were about to walk out the door, my phone buzzed. I looked at the screen and frowned. "It's the chief," I said. "Why is he calling me and not you?"

"The chief works in wondrous ways," she said, "the reasons for which he keeps to himself," she replied. "You'd better answer it."

So I did.

"Harry, I need you and Kate back here now. Mornay and Collins as well. Tell 'em!" And then, before I could speak, he hung up.

I looked at Kate. She was grinning. "He wants us back, like now, right?"

I nodded as I shoved my phone back into my jacket pocket.

"He's changed since you left the force," she said, "and not for the better, I sometimes think. We'd better do as he says. We can get something to eat later. What about them?" She nodded toward the two agents.

"Yup, them too," I replied.

Thirty minutes later, Kate and I, along with Agents Collins and Mornay, were sitting in the chief's office, listening as he recounted Victoria's escalating desperation and the systematic destruction of her criminal network.

"Victoria Ashcroft held a press conference yesterday afternoon," Johnston said, starting a video on his computer. "She's going public with her version of events."

The video showed Victoria standing behind a podium in what appeared to be a hotel conference room. She was flanked by lawyers and surrounded by reporters. She looked composed and professional, but I could see signs of strain around her eyes, the kind of stress that comes from knowing your entire world is collapsing around you.

"Ladies and gentlemen," Victoria began, "I'm here today to address the false accusations and unfounded speculation that have been directed at Ashcroft Chemical and myself personally over the past month."

She spoke for nearly ten minutes, denying any involvement in illegal dumping, characterizing the environmental research as biased and unscientific, and suggesting that the recent murders were the work of environmental extremists trying to frame her and her company for crimes they didn't commit.

"She's trying to control the narrative," Collins said as the video ended. "Classic crisis management strategy: get your version of events out before the prosecution can present their evidence."

"But she made a crucial mistake," Agent Mornay added, rewinding the video to a specific section. "Look at this part of her statement."

She replayed a section where Victoria discussed the recent deaths. "The tragic murders of Dr. Jones, Commissioner Walsh, Mr. Murdoch, attorney Robert Crane and now the break in at my offices and the death of Randolf Webb, our CEO, represent a systematic campaign of violence against anyone associated with environmental policy in this region."

"She mentioned Crane's murder," Kate said immediately. "But that information—that he was murdered—wasn't released to the media."

"Which proves nothing," I said testily. "Crane was Victoria's attorney, for Pete's sake. Anyone could and would have told her: Crane's secretary or any one of her staff, not to mention the leak in this task force."

Mornay looked chastened. Kate simply raised her eyebrows and nodded. Neither of them spoke.

"There's more," Johnston said, pulling up additional files on his computer. "After the press conference, Victoria disappeared. No one on her staff knows where she is. She's not at home, and her personal security detail was dismissed yesterday evening."

"She's running," Kate said.

"Or she's planning something," I replied. "Someone who's been willing to commit murder to protect a criminal enterprise doesn't usually just give up and flee. They escalate."

Agent Collins spread out several surveillance photos on the chief's desk. "These were taken yesterday evening, near the old Ashcroft Chemical plant. As you can see, there are several vehicles on site, and personnel moving around the facility. The plant was completely cleaned out; there's nothing there except empty buildings, so what's going on? Could it be they're planning something, that Victoria's planning something? "

I studied the photographs. Even in the grainy surveillance images, I could see there were more than a dozen people, most of them wearing what looked to me like body armor, moving purposefully around the empty facility, setting up lights and what appeared to be staging areas and, according to the timestamps, working under floodlights well into the night.

"I think maybe she's going back to where it all started," I said.

"But why?" Kate asked. "The facility's been empty for weeks. There's no evidence left to destroy."

"Maybe there's something we missed," Mornay suggested. "Some crucial piece of evidence that could expose the entire operation."

"There's nothing there," I said. "If there had been, Samson would have found it. No, she's up to something, and whatever it is, I guarantee she's up to no good.."

"Harry, Kate," Johnston said. "I've got teams on their way to the chemical plant now. I've told them to hold and wait for us before they enter the perimeter. Get out of here. Go see what's going on, but be careful. She's a killer, and if she's planning something… this could be extremely dangerous."

And we did.

It was some ten minutes later as we were preparing to leave for the chemical plant when Collins pulled us aside.

"There's something else you need to know," he said quietly. "I just got word that another forty million dollars has been transferred out of Victoria's accounts in the past forty-eight hours. That makes sixty million. Either she's preparing to disappear permanently, or she's funding something that requires massive resources."

"Like hiring a private army," I replied. "Look at the photos."

"Then you'd better do as the chief says and be careful," he said. "My tactical units are already on the way."

"We already are," I replied with a smile, tapping the ceramic plate in the vest I was wearing. "'Careful' is my middle name."

———

THE DRIVE to the old Ashcroft Chemical plant took us through the industrial corridor west of Chattanooga, past abandoned factories and overgrown lots, the remnants of the city's complicated relationship with environmental protection and economic development.

It was just after ten that Thursday morning—and we still hadn't eaten—as we approached the chemical plant. We could see light poles, what looked like several light armored vehicles parked in various locations around the property, and there was still some activity that confirmed the surveillance reports.

"Geez," Kate said, studying the scene through binoculars. "You were right, Harry. This looks like a military operation." And instinctively, she shortened Samson's leash.

By then, Collins had joined us and was coordinating his tactical units positioned at a discrete distance around the perimeter.

"We've got eyes on at least a dozen people inside the facility," he said. "They're not military, or locals. I think they're private security contractors."

"Why am I not surprised?" I asked.

My phone buzzed with a call from TJ. "Harry, I'm positioned on the bluff overlooking the plant. You need to know there's someone else here. I can see them. They're also watching the facility."

"Can you identify them?" I asked.

"Negative. Too far away."

"Stay on it, TJ. See if you can get close enough to identify them."

"Can't do it, Harry. I already tried. There's a fast-running creek between me and them."

"Well, just… keep an eye on them, then."

Kate's radio crackled, "Captain, there's something

happening on the west side of the main building. There are four huge tanker trucks at the rear of the building. It looks like they're preparing to pump whatever's in them into the river."

"She's planning one last massive dump," I said. "If she does, it will pollute the river for miles downstream."

"Or she's planning to destroy the facility and everyone in it," Kate replied grimly.

"I don't think Victoria's planning to run," I said.

"Then what?" Collins asked.

"Hell, I don't know," I replied. "The woman's in a panic. She could do anything, including industrial blackmail, though that would be a desperate, but futile last stand. No, I think she has to get rid of whatever's in those tankers before Mornay's people seize them. Which means we have to move, and move quickly."

"Agent Collins," a voice said over his radio, "we've got movement toward the facility. Someone's approaching on foot from the river access road."

I grabbed Kate's binoculars and focused on the lone figure walking purposefully toward the main entrance. I frowned, continued watching for a long moment. There was something familiar about the gait, the posture—

"That's not one of Victoria's security contractors," Kate said, interrupting my thoughts as she tried to take the binoculars back.

I shrugged her off. "Give me a minute," I snapped. Then continued to watch as the figure approached the main gate. And as the person glanced round, and I caught a glimpse of her profile. "What the hell...?" I muttered. "No, it can't be... But it is." I stared at the figure for another long moment, then said, "Kate," I said, "I know who that is." And I handed her the binoculars.

"Who?" she asked, taking them from me.

"Dr. Sally Howard," I replied.

"You're kidding," she snapped as she raised the binoculars. "Are you sure?"

"Oh yeah. I'm sure."

14

Dark Waters

Friday, Week 4

It was two o'clock at the old Ashcroft Chemical plant that Thursday afternoon, and we were at the point where the confrontation we'd been building toward for almost a month was upon us. But, as the tactical units repositioned themselves around the facility, and we watched the person I thought to be Sally Howard approach the main entrance, my phone rang with the call I'd been waiting for since Dr. Jennifer Parker's body was discovered in the sea turtle tank.

"Harry," Doc Sheddon's familiar voice sounded hollow through the speaker, "I need to speak with you and Captain Gazzara immediately. I've been reviewing the pathology work done while I was away, and there are serious problems with several conclusions, the most problematic being that of Dr. Parker."

"Doc, we're in the middle of a tactical operation here," I said, watching through binoculars as Victoria's security contractors maintained their positions around the chemical plant. "Can this wait?"

"No, it cannot," he replied firmly. "The autopsy conclusions for Dr. Parker are inaccurate, and if you're planning to arrest someone based on those findings, you're going to have serious problems in court."

Kate grabbed my phone. "Doc, this is Kate. What kind of problems?"

"The kind that could get murder charges thrown out of court," he said. "Dr. Hensley's time of death estimate for Dr. Parker is wrong by several hours. I have the proof."

Kate and I looked at each other. I nodded. I knew exactly what she was thinking. If Doc could prove that Victoria's alibi didn't cover the time of Parker's murder, her alibi was no good.

"Doc," Kate said, "how certain are you about this?"

"Excuse me, young lady. I don't make these kind of mistakes. How certain am I? I'm absolutely certain. I returned from my conference yesterday and spent all night reviewing every aspect of the autopsy, consulting with experts at Vanderbilt, and having the toxicology results verified by independent laboratories. Dr. Parker died much later than Dr. Hensley claimed."

Agent Collins, who'd been monitoring our conversation, said, "What you're saying is that if the time of death is wrong, then Victoria Ashcroft's alibi is worthless," he said.

"Exactly," Kate said, gifting Collins with a wry glance. "Doc, what's the correct time of death?"

"Based on stomach content analysis, water temperature effects, and rigor mortis patterns in aquatic environments, Dr. Parker died between ten o'clock and midnight Saturday night, not nine to ten-thirty as Dr. Hensley states in her report."

So, the pieces were finally clicking into place. "Victoria's charity event ended at eleven that night, and if Dr. Parker died sometime between ten and midnight, Victoria doesn't have an alibi for between eleven and midnight."

"And there's more," Doc continued over the phone. "I found traces of sedative in Dr. Parker's system that Dr. Hensley either missed or ignored. Someone drugged Dr. Parker before injecting her with tetrodotoxin."

Kate was already coordinating with the district attorney's office by phone. The corrected timeline, combined with Sally Howard's identification of Victoria as her attacker, would finally provide enough evidence to arrest Victoria on suspicion of Dr. Parker's murder.

But before we could process the implications of Doc's findings, Agent Collins received an urgent radio transmission that changed our priorities.

"Sir, the tanker trucks are moving into position near the river access. It looks like they're preparing to pump."

"They're going to dump everything into the river," Agent Mornay said. "If those tankers contain the concentrated chemical waste we suspect, they could contaminate the Tennessee River system for hundreds of miles downstream. We have to do something now!"

"All units, move now," Collins broadcast over the radio. "The priority is to secure those tanker trucks before any chemicals can be released. The secondary objective is to neutralize the security contractors and detain Victoria Ashcoft."

Kate, Samson, and I moved with the tactical teams as they advanced on the chemical plant. We followed the FBI armored transporter as it smashed through the front gate, and the facility erupted into controlled chaos as the SWAT officers surrounded the tanker trucks while other teams moved to apprehend Victoria's mercenaries.

"Federal agents! Drop your weapons!" echoed across the facility as FBI and EPA tactical officers swarmed the compound.

The security contractors, despite their professional appearance, surrendered without resistance when faced with overwhelming federal firepower. Not a shot was fired and, within minutes, a dozen heavily armed mercenaries were on the ground in zip-tie restraints while EPA hazmat specialists began securing the tanker trucks.

"Harry, Kate," Collins called over the radio, "we've secured the perimeter and the environmental threat, but we've lost visual on the primary target. Victoria Ashcroft is somewhere inside the main building."

"And so is our lone walker," I replied, remembering the figure we'd seen approaching the facility. "Someone else is in there with Victoria."

Kate and I approached what once had been the main laboratory building with Sammy straining at the leash along with tactical backup, moving throughout the industrial complex that had been the center of Victoria's illegal dumping operation. The concrete structures and rusted storage tanks created a maze of potential hiding places and ambush points.

Once inside, we could hear voices echoing through the empty building from the upper levels. It sounded as if some sort of confrontation was already in progress.

"This way," Kate said, following the sound with Samson

still straining at the leash, leading us through the facility. "They're in the chemical processing area."

We climbed a metal staircase to the second floor, where rusting catwalks and processing equipment created a complex industrial landscape some forty feet above a fast-running sluice that carried water through the facility into the Tennessee River. As we approached, the sound of voices arguing grew louder.

"You killed her," someone shouted, "the woman I loved." The familiar voice was filled with cold fury.

Dr. Sally Howard stood on one of the catwalks, a gun in one hand and a syringe in the other, holding Victoria Ashcroft at gunpoint near the edge of the platform. Victoria was backed up against the catwalk railing, her hands in the air, her face pale with terror as she stared at the woman who had systematically destroyed her entire criminal network.

"Drop your weapon!" Kate shouted, her gun drawn but lowered. "Dr. Howard, drop the weapon and step away from Victoria!"

Sally looked at us calmly, showing no surprise at our arrival. "Hello, Captain Gazzara, Harry. Stay away. Back off. I'm not done here. "

"Sally," I said gently, "you don't have to do this. We have enough evidence to convict Victoria of Jennifer's murder. Doc Sheddon proved her alibi doesn't hold up."

But do we have enough evidence? I thought *breaking her alibi is one thing; proving she actually killed Dr. Parker is quite another.*

"Dr. Sheddon," Sally laughed bitterly. "If he'd been here from the beginning instead of that corrupt hospital patholo-gist, Jennifer's killer would have been arrested weeks ago. Instead, Victoria's been free to destroy evidence and eliminate witnesses while I watched everyone involved in the conspiracy go unpunished."

"So you took justice into your own hands," Kate said.

"Justice for Jenny, yes! You could even say I was seeking revenge," Sally said. "But no matter how you put it, it's well deserved. Justice would have been Victoria in prison for life. Revenge is making sure she pays for what she did to Jennifer."

Victoria finally found her voice. "Please," she said desperately, "I can give you money, information, anything you want. I never meant for Dr. Parker to die. She threatened to expose everything I'd worked for: the business, the contracts, the financial arrangements. I had to protect myself."

"Protect yourself?" Sally yelled. "You injected Jennifer with tetrodotoxin. You paralyzed her and threw her into that tank to drown while she was still conscious and aware. That's not self-defense; that's torture."

"Please don't kill me," Victoria said desperately. "Yes, I admit it. I killed Jennifer Parker. I also killed my father fifteen years ago when he threatened to expose the dumping operation. I've killed EPA inspectors, environmental activists, anyone who threatened my business. But Sally, you've killed almost as many people as I have."

"I killed criminals," Sally replied coldly. "Jones was feeding you intelligence about environmental research. Walsh was providing political protection in exchange for bribes. Crane was structuring your legal defenses. Murdoch was issuing false paperwork to cover your crimes against the environment; Webb was managing your illegal operations. And I tried to kill Muldoon and Marsh. They all enabled your crimes, and they all paid the price."

Kate moved closer, her weapon still lowered, and I knew her plan was to keep her talking. "Sally, how did you get access to tetrodotoxin? How did you know about Victoria's financial network?"

"I'm a marine biologist, Captain. Extracting and preparing neurotoxins is part of my expertise. As for Victoria's network, Jennifer shared everything with me. When Victoria killed her, I used that information to destroy everyone who had enabled Victoria's crimes."

"What about Dr. Hensley?" I asked.

Sally smiled grimly. "That corrupt bitch was next on my list. She'd been taking payments from Victoria for years. I knew she must have manipulated the autopsy results to give Victoria an alibi for Jennifer's murder."

"Then why didn't you bring it to my attention?" Kate asked.

"Because I needed time to eliminate her entire network," Sally replied. "If Victoria had been arrested immediately for Jennifer's murder, her associates would have scattered or destroyed evidence. I wanted them all to pay for enabling her crimes."

Victoria seized on the conversation as an opportunity to edge away from Sally along the catwalk. "You see?" she said desperately. "Sally's the real killer here. She's murdered five people."

"You're right," Sally said calmly. "I killed those people. I used your sympathy for my loss to deflect suspicion from me, and it worked. And it would have continued to work if this stupid woman hadn't decided to dump catastrophic quantities of chemical waste into the river. I couldn't let that happen. So I tried to stop her, but she'd already given the order, and then the silly bitch managed to drop her phone somewhere while I was chasing her. I was too late. Thank God you arrived when you did. The consequences of the dump would have killed the wildlife for hundreds of miles downstream. So I guess some good will come of all this."

As Sally spoke, Victoria continued to move crabwise along the catwalk toward what appeared to be another staircase. But the railing was corroded and unstable, and the industrial platform was slick with decades of chemical residue.

"Victoria," I shouted, "stop. That railing won't hold your weight."

But Victoria, driven by panic and desperation, was beyond rational thought. She grabbed the railing and tried to climb over it, apparently planning to drop to a lower platform or access ladder.

The corroded metal rail gave way with a screeching sound of twisted steel. Victoria screamed and let go of the rail, but it was too late. She fell backward, arms spread wide, screaming, a long wailing screech as she fell, tumbling, her arms flailing, forty feet into the fast-running sluice below, her scream cut short as she hit the fast-moving water, fed by the recent rains and the run-off from the mountain, and was swept away, face up. Within seconds, Victoria's body was gone, carried away by the rushing water toward the Tennessee River.

"Oh my God," Kate muttered, as she rushed to the edge of the platform.

Me? I simply stood and watched Victoria's body now tumbling in the current as it was carried toward the river system she had spent so many years poisoning. The irony of it was not lost on me: Victoria Ashcroft was being washed away by the very waterways she'd contaminated.

"Sally," Kate said, turning back to Dr. Howard, "you can put the gun and the syringe down now. It's over."

"Yes," Sally said quietly, "it is over." She set them down on the platform and raised her hands. "Victoria's dead, her network is destroyed, and the truth about Jennifer's murder has been exposed. I'm ready for what's going to happen to me."

As Kate's officers took Sally into custody, Agent Collins coordinated the recovery efforts for Victoria's body. But the current was strong, and by the time the Tennessee Wildlife boats reached the area where she'd entered the river proper, there was no sign of her.

"We'll continue searching downstream," Collins said, "but with this current, recovery may be difficult."

As evening fell over the Tennessee River, the local hazmat specialists continued securing the four tanker trucks while federal agents processed the facility for evidence. Though knowing what had happened there over the past several weeks, I knew there was little left to find, and I told Collins so, but his attitude was better safe than sorry, and I suppose he was right.

The big deal was, of course, that the environmental threat had been prevented, Victoria's mercenary army was in custody, and both killers—Victoria and Sally—had been identified and dealt with, though Victoria's body hadn't yet been recovered.

The fast-running sluice and swirling currents as it entered the Tennessee made recovery impossible, and despite extensive search efforts, Victoria Ashcroft had disappeared into the river system. Whether she had drowned or somehow survived remained an open question.

"Kate," I said as we prepared to leave the chemical plant, "do you think Victoria's really dead?"

"With that fall and that current?" Kate replied. "She'd have to be superhuman to survive. But until we find a body, there's always going to be doubt."

Doc Sheddon met us at the facility's entrance, having driven directly from his office with the corrected autopsy findings that had finally broken Victoria's alibi for Jennifer's murder.

"So it's over, then?" Doc asked as he watched the first tanker being driven away.

"Mostly," I replied. "We've got Sally Howard in custody, but Victoria fell from the catwalk into the sluice and was swept away. That and we've prevented a massive environmental disaster."

"And Dr. Parker's murder?" he asked.

"Victoria confessed before she fell," Kate said. "She even confessed to killing her own father, so now, with that and your corrected timeline, we can close that case. As for the rest of the murders and the attacks on Frank Muldoon and Eddie Marsh, Sally Howard confessed to those. The only thing left in doubt is the attack on Michael Drake, and I have to assume that Victoria was responsible for that one, too. After all, she would have been the one to benefit from his death."

Doc paused for a moment before answering, obviously mulling things over as he watched the hazmat team finishing up their work. Then he said, "You know, Harry, in my forty years of doing this job, I've seen a lot of evil, but this... this was something else entirely. The calculated nature of it, the way Victoria killed her own father, then Dr. Parker..." He shook his head and then continued, "The tetrodotoxin was a clever choice. It would make drowning the obvious conclusion if you didn't know what to look for."

Doc turned his head to look directly at me. "At least now those families will have some closure. Dr. Parker's parents, the others... they'll know their loved ones didn't die for nothing. Victoria would have continued to pollute the river, had not

Dr. Parker been brave enough, not only to investigate it but also to confront her." He shook his head again. "I just wish we could have saved more of them."

"Thanks, Doc," I said. "You're a blessing."

He smiled. "I think that may be a bridge too far, Harry. But on that note, I'll leave you. Stay safe, both of you." And he turned and walked away.

As we drove back toward Chattanooga, I couldn't help but think about the complex motivations that had driven the two killers. Victoria had murdered to protect a criminal enterprise worth millions of dollars. Sally had murdered to avenge the woman she loved and to destroy the network that had enabled Victoria's crimes. It was hard to believe that two highly educated women could resort to murder the way they had. It truly was one for the books.

"Harry," Kate said as we crossed the bridge over the Tennessee River, "what do you think about what Sally did? Was she justified?"

"Of course not," I said. "You know better than to ask me that, Kate. Sally thinks she was justified, though. She loved Jennifer, and she wanted to see justice done. But justice isn't the same as revenge, and murder isn't the same as justice. Murder can never be justified, not under any circumstances."

"Even when the system fails to provide justice?" Kate asked.

"Especially then," I said. "Because once we start executing people without a trial, we become the criminals we're trying to stop."

The Hunter's Moon had set, taking with it the complex web of murder and environmental crime that had consumed our investigation. But it had also taught us something about the thin line between justice and revenge, and the dangerous territory we enter when grief and anger overcome our commitment to the rule of law.

Dr. Jennifer Parker's murder was finally solved, but at the cost of six more lives, if you include Victoria's, and the near-destruction of the very environment she had died trying to protect. Food for thought indeed.

15

Red Tide

Saturday, Week 4

SATURDAY MORNING BROUGHT THE KIND OF EXHAUSTION THAT settles deep into your bones after a case that's consumed every waking moment for a month. It was just after eight o'clock, and I was sitting in my home office staring at crime scene photographs spread across my desk, when the last pieces of the puzzle finally clicked into place.

Amanda found me there an hour later, asleep at my desk, surrounded by the files.

"Harry, you've been in here since five o'clock," she said, putting her hand on my shoulder as she set a cup of coffee beside me. "What are you doing? The case is solved. Dr. Howard's in custody and Victoria's... Well, God only knows what's happened to her. You should be celebrating, not torturing yourself like this."

"Amanda," I said, pointing to a surveillance photograph from the Ashcroft Chemical parking lot, "look at this image from last Tuesday. The day Marcus Webb was murdered."

She studied the photograph, then looked at me frowning. "Okay, it's a parking lot. What am I supposed to see?"

"Look at this car," I said, pointing to a dark sedan partially visible in the background. "Now look at this traffic camera footage Tim pulled from the same day."

I showed her a series of time-stamped images from traffic cameras around the chemical plant. The same dark sedan appeared in multiple locations throughout the day, following a pattern that placed it near the building during the exact window when Webb was murdered.

"Someone was conducting surveillance on Webb," she said.

"Not someone," I replied, pulling out more photographs. "Sally Howard. Tim identified the license plate this morning. It's registered to her."

Amanda sat down heavily in the chair across from my desk. "You think she was stalking her victims before killing them?"

"Yeah, it's damn obvious now," I replied as I showed her the timeline I'd been constructing since before dawn. "Every murder was planned weeks in advance. Sally researched her victims' schedules, habits, and vulnerabilities. She knew exactly when and where to strike for maximum effect."

"But that's what you'd expect from someone conducting a revenge campaign," Amanda said.

"True. But look at this," I said, showing her the financial records that Tim had discovered in Sally's university computer. "She either hacked Victoria's bank accounts, or someone did it for her."

Amanda studied the banking records with growing

amazement. "She stole sixty million dollars from Victoria's accounts?"

"She did," I replied. "Sixty million dollars were transferred from Victoria's offshore accounts to a half-dozen environmental protection organizations, including the World Wildlife Fund, the Sierra Club, Greenpeace, and the Tennessee River-keeper. How frickin' ironic is that? Sally turned Victoria's criminal profits into environmental protection funding."

"So she wasn't just seeking revenge," Amanda said slowly. "She was conducting financial warfare against the entire operation."

My phone buzzed with a call from Kate. "Harry, you need to get down here immediately. Sally's asking for you."

"She is?" I looked up at Amanda. She shrugged.

"She says she'll only provide a full confession if she can speak with you first. She says she's got something she wants to tell you she won't share with anyone else. Her lawyer's agreed, but Harry…?"

I sighed, took a sip of my now almost cooled coffee, and said, "Give me an hour."

An hour later, I was sitting across from Dr. Sally Howard and her attorney in an interview room at the police department on Amnicola Highway. And my first thought as I sat down was that she looked remarkably composed for someone facing multiple murder charges. I also noticed a look in her eyes that suggested she still might have cards to play.

"Hello, Harry," she said calmly. "Thank you for coming."

"Sally," I replied, "Captain Gazzara tells me you want to make a confession."

"A confession?" She shrugged, made a face, then said, "Yes, I suppose you could call it that. But what I really want is to tell you the truth about what I've been doing for the past month," she said. "Because I think you're the only investigator involved in this case who might actually understand my motivations."

Kate was monitoring the interview from the observation room next door, along with Agent Collins.

I glanced at Sally's attorney, a sharp-looking woman named Patricia Brennan, who specialized in federal criminal defense.

"All right," I said, "so tell me the truth."

Sally leaned back in her chair, her expression thoughtful. "When Victoria killed Jennifer, she didn't just murder the woman I loved. She destroyed the most important environmental research being conducted in this region. Jennifer's work could have saved the Tennessee River system and prevented decades of additional contamination."

"So you decided to destroy Victoria's entire operation," I said.

"I decided to do what Jennifer would have wanted," Sally replied. "Expose the crimes, eliminate the criminals, and use Victoria's own resources to fund environmental protection efforts wherever they might be needed."

She paused, studying my face for reaction. "Harry, Jennifer shared everything with me. Not just her research, but her fears about the scope of Victoria's criminal network. She knew Victoria had been systematically corrupting officials, bribing inspectors, and eliminating threats for more than a decade and a half."

"Including murdering her own father," I said, encouraging her to keep talking.

Sally nodded. "Jennifer had evidence that Victoria killed William Ashcroft to prevent him from exposing the illegal dumping operation. But she needed more proof before she could present her findings to federal authorities."

"Which is why she confronted Victoria at the aquarium," I said.

"Jennifer believed that by showing her the evidence, she could convince Victoria to stop what she was doing. That was Jenny. Ever the optimist, but she was naïve about how dangerous Victoria had become." Sally's voice grew harder. "Victoria didn't just kill Jennifer; she tortured her. The tetrodotoxin paralyzed Jennifer while leaving her conscious and aware of what was happening to her. Can you even imagine what that must have been like for her? Victoria wanted her to suffer, as she must have done."

I thought about the crime scene at the aquarium, the way Dr. Parker's body had been positioned in the tank. "How do you know these details?"

"I know because Victoria told me," Sally said quietly. "During our confrontation at the chemical plant, before you arrived and so rudely interrupted us. She was proud of what she'd done. She said Jennifer got what she deserved."

"Harry, ask her about the murders," Kate said through my earpiece.

"Sally," I said, "tell me about Jones, Walsh, Crane, Murdoch and Webb. Why did you kill them?"

Sally's expression changed to one of anger. "Each of them played a specific role in enabling Victoria's crimes. Jones was feeding Victoria intelligence about environmental research at the aquarium. Walsh was providing political protection in exchange for campaign contributions. Murdoch was supplying fake documents. Crane structured the legal frame-work that allowed Victoria to operate with impunity. And

Webb was managing the operational aspects of the illegal dumping."

"And Muldoon and Marsh?" I asked.

"Come on, Harry. You know why. They were doing the actual dumping and getting well paid for it too."

"So you eliminated them one by one," I said.

"All but Muldoon and Marsh, yes," she replied. "Unfortunately, I wasn't quite good enough to end those two river pirates, more's the pity. The others? I researched them extensively: their schedules, their habits, their vulnerabilities. I wanted to understand exactly how Victoria's network functioned before I destroyed it."

She opened a notebook that her attorney had brought to the interview. "This contains detailed profiles of everyone involved in Victoria's operation. Financial records, personal information, evidence of their crimes."

I studied the notebook, amazed by the thoroughness of Sally's investigation. She had compiled information that would have taken federal agencies months to gather.

"How did you access Victoria's financial accounts?" I asked.

"Jennifer had been tracking Victoria's money laundering operations as part of her environmental research," Sally replied. "She needed to understand the financial incentives behind the illegal dumping. When Victoria killed her, I used Jennifer's research and... a friend to drain Victoria's accounts."

"And you stole sixty million dollars," I said.

Sally smiled for the first time during our conversation. "Stole?" She said, her brow wrinkled. "You could put it that way, I suppose. But it was tainted money. Ill-gotten gains for which Victoria spent decades poisoning the environment. I thought it would be appropriate that I should put those ill-gotten gains to good use and fund some good causes."

Kate's voice came through my earpiece again. "Ask her about Dr. Hensley."

"Sally, what was your relationship with Dr. Hensley? How did you convince her to provide false autopsy results?"

Sally's expression became distant, calculating. "I didn't. That was Victoria. Dr. Hensley has been accepting bribes from Victoria for years to manipulate autopsy results. I simply documented her corruption. She was next on my list, by the way."

I was beginning to understand the sophistication of Sally's plan. She had manipulated the entire investigation to achieve her objectives.

"Sally," I said, "you used us. You used us, didn't you?"

She smiled. "I used your investigation to seek justice for Jennifer," she replied. "The legal system was too slow, too corrupt, too easily manipulated by people like Victoria. I took direct action to ensure that everyone responsible for Jennifer's death faced consequences."

"Sally," I said, leaning forward, "you've been remarkably well-informed about our investigation. You knew exactly what we were doing and when we were doing it. My question is, how did you know?"

Sally's expression became calculating. "What do you mean?"

"I mean, someone was feeding you information about the task force's activities. The timing of your actions was too precise to be coincidental. You knew when to move against Victoria's network, when to destroy evidence, when we were closing in."

Sally smiled coldly, tilted her head slightly to the left and said, "Dr. Hensley."

I heard Kate gasp through my earpiece.

"Patricia Hensley was working with you?" I asked, stunned by the revelation. "But she was responsible for Victoria's alibi?"

"That was the beauty and the irony of it," she replied. "I knew no one would suspect her. I also knew that as an informal part of the task force, she could stay current with everything you were doing. She became my spy."

"But why would she do that?" I asked.

"Patricia was terrified of me," Sally replied matter-of-factly. "I had documentation of her taking bribes from Victoria to falsify autopsy results. I confronted her, showed her what I had, and she realized I could destroy her career and send her to prison. So I simply blackmailed her."

"So how did it work?" I asked.

"She received copies of the minutes of each task force meeting, and she called me if there'd been any significant developments. Patricia knew I'd eventually send her to prison—which I have, haven't I? Anyway, she was desperately trying to buy herself time by being useful to me." There was no sympathy in Sally's voice. "She thought if she helped me eliminate Victoria's network, I might spare her. Fat chance!"

"So you were never going to... spare her?" I said.

"Of course not," Sally replied. "Patricia enabled Victoria's crimes. She deserved the same fate as the rest of them. Now she'll get what's coming to her."

Collins' voice came through my earpiece. "Harry, ask her about the chemical plant confrontation. Was she planning to kill Victoria and then herself?"

"Sally, what was your plan for the confrontation with Victoria? Were you planning a murder-suicide?"

Sally was quiet for a long moment, her expression thoughtful. "Suicide? Me? Of course not. I was planning to give Victoria the same death she gave Jennifer. Paralyzed, conscious, aware of what was happening. Then I was planning to get out of there, but you put a stop to that, didn't you? "

"I don't understand," I said. I did, but I wanted her to tell me. "Why didn't you go to the authorities, Sally? You could even have come to me."

Sally shook her head. "I didn't trust the legal system to convict Victoria. She had too many connections, too much money, too many ways to manipulate the process. I wanted to ensure justice for Jennifer."

Kate entered the interview room, taking a seat beside me. "Dr. Howard, we need you to make a full statement of your activities during the past month."

Sally nodded. "Ah yes, the confession. I can do that. I'll provide you with a complete confession, including detailed information about Victoria's criminal network, the environmental crimes, and the systematic corruption of local officials."

"In exchange for what?" Kate asked.

"Nothing," Sally replied. "I simply want the truth to be known. I want Jennifer's research to be vindicated. I want Victoria's crimes to be fully exposed and prosecuted. I want to talk to the press." She looked at me and said, "I'm sure you can arrange that, Mr. Starke."

Sally's attorney leaned forward. "My client is prepared to plead guilty to all charges in exchange for cooperation with federal authorities in prosecuting the environmental crimes and corruption cases."

Over the next four hours, Sally provided the most comprehensive confession I'd ever witnessed. She detailed every aspect of her revenge campaign, her financial warfare against Victoria's operation, her manipulation of our investigation, and her research into Victoria's criminal network.

She explained how she had used her university credentials to access research databases, her marine biology expertise to prepare tetrodotoxin, and her knowledge of Jennifer's research to identify everyone involved in the conspiracy.

"I studied each target extensively," she said, showing us detailed files provided by her attorney. "I knew their schedules, their habits, their vulnerabilities. I wanted to eliminate them efficiently while gathering intelligence about Victoria's operation."

She had documented everything.

"I think Jennifer would have been proud of the thoroughness of my investigation," Sally said. "I used her research to expose the very crimes that led to her death."

As afternoon turned to evening, we completed Sally's confession and began the process of verifying her claims. The evidence she provided was overwhelming.

"Harry," Kate said as we prepared to leave, "it's stunning, the way she went about it. I've never seen anything like it. She would have made a terrific detective."

I was silent for a long moment, then said, "I never met Jennifer Parker, but I can't believe she would have approved of what Sally did. She virtually manipulated our investigation to achieve her own objectives," I replied. "Every time we interviewed her, she was gathering intelligence about our progress while deflecting suspicion from herself. That aside, she's a calculating, cold-blooded killer."

"But in so doing she exposed Victoria's crimes and redirected sixty million dollars to environmental protection," Kate pointed out. "And, as far as I know, it's going to be difficult to get any of it back."

"At the cost of five lives," I said. "There's no way to justify that, no matter how sophisticated the method. Kate, she executed those people."

Kate didn't answer, and we rode the elevator to the second floor in silence. The elevator doors opened, and we stepped out into an unusually quiet situation room.

"Kate," I said, as we walked across the room to her office, "you don't really think Sally's actions were justified, do you?"

"I think Sally loved Jennifer and wanted to see her killers punished," Kate replied. "But murder is still murder, regardless of the motivation. So no, I don't."

"Not even when the victims were criminals themselves?" I asked, smiling.

"Especially then," Kate said. "Because, to paraphrase you, once we start executing people without a trial, we become the criminals we're trying to stop."

My phone buzzed with a call from Amanda. "Harry, I've been watching the news coverage of the arrests. Channel 7 is reporting that Sally Howard redirected sixty million dollars from Victoria's accounts to environmental organizations. Is that true?"

"It's true," I replied. "Sally turned Victoria's profits into environmental protection funding."

"Wow, that's really something. There has to be a story in there for me. I want the exclusive, Harry."

I smiled to myself. I had her on speaker, so Kate could hear too.

"I'm sure there will be an official press release," Kate said. "But yes, I'll see if I can talk the chief into it, and I'm willing to bet, after what we've just been through, that Sally will be more than cooperative. "

"That would be amazing," Amanda replied. "D'you really think you can arrange it, Kate?"

"I'll do my best," she replied, and winked at me.

Agents Collins and Mornay were waiting for us in Kate's office. Samson ran to Collins as we entered and nuzzled his hand.

"We've not found Victoria's body," he said. "And, looking at that river beyond Racoon Mountain, I'm not surprised. If we do find her alive, she'll be charged with murder, conspiracy to commit environmental crimes, bribery, money laundering, and about fifteen other federal offenses," he said. "The evidence Sally provided will make conviction a virtual certainty."

"What about the environmental cleanup?" Kate asked.

"The EPA is initiating a massive remediation effort for the Tennessee River system," Mornay said.

As evening fell that final Saturday, I was back in my home office, reviewing the evidence one last time and then packing it away. The photographs, financial records, and confession documents painted a picture of two very different killers: Victoria, who murdered to protect criminal profits, and Sally Howard, who murdered to seek justice for environmental crimes and personal loss. Victoria? Did she deserve her fate? I can't tell you. I'm not the person to judge her. I leave that to those better qualified, and ultimately to the Lord. Sally Howard? Same answer, but I must admit to feeling a little sympathy for her. Don't ask me why.

Amanda joined me as I was closing the files. "So, it's over, then. How do you feel about it?" she asked.

"Happy," I replied. "But I don't want to talk about it."

"I understand," she said. "So, come on. Let's have dinner together. It's been a while."

And we did.

The Hunter's Moon case was finally closed. It had been one of the most perplexing cases I'd ever undertaken, be it only as a consultant. But along the way, I'd discovered that justice isn't always about who's wearing the badge. Sometimes it's about who's willing to pay the price, and in this case, the price had been measured in lives rather than years behind bars.

16

Clear Waters

Six Months Later

I DON'T KNOW IF IT WAS JUST ME, BUT AS I LOOKED OUT OVER the river on a sunny Wednesday morning six months after we put the Hunter's Moon case to bed, it seemed to me it looked different in the late spring sunlight, flowing clean and purposefully past the Tennessee Aquarium. Yes, it had been six months, and the scars were finally beginning to heal, both for the river and for those of us who had lived through the investigation.

"Daddy, can we see Neptune again?" Jade asked, tugging on my sleeve as she finished her ice cream cone.

"Of course, princess," I said, standing and taking her small hand in mine. "That's why we're here."

The aquarium had reopened three months earlier after extensive renovations and the installation of enhanced security. The Neptune exhibit had been completely rebuilt, with new filtration systems, improved access controls, and a memorial plaque dedicated to Dr. Jennifer Parker's environmental research. No one would say where the money to do it came from, but I could guess.

As we walked through the familiar galleries, I thought about how much had changed since that restless October night when Kate and I had first discovered Dr. Parker's body floating in the sea turtle habitat. The case that had started with a single murder had ultimately exposed a criminal enterprise spanning more than a decade and had led to the largest environmental prosecution in Tennessee history.

"Harry," Amanda said, linking her arm through mine as we approached the Neptune exhibit, "you've been quiet all morning. What's on your mind?"

"I was just thinking about how it all ended," I replied.

The new Neptune exhibit was magnificent. The rescued green sea turtle swam majestically through crystal-clear water, surrounded by vibrant coral formations and tropical fish. A new placard explained Neptune's rescue story and the importance of protecting marine ecosystems from pollution and contamination.

But what caught my attention was the memorial plaque mounted beside the exhibit:

In memory of Dr. Jennifer Parker (1987-2025) environmental scientist, researcher, and advocate, her dedication to protecting aquatic ecosystems continues to inspire conservation efforts throughout the Tennessee River system.

Jade pressed her face against the acrylic glass, watching Neptune glide through the water with the graceful power that had made him a beloved fixture at the aquarium for over a decade.

"He looks happy, Daddy," she said.

"Yes, he does," I agreed, remembering the distressed turtle we'd found circling Dr. Parker's body six months ago.

I looked at Amanda. She smiled.

It was a little more than an hour later, at a little after two-thirty, that my phone buzzed with a text from Kate: *The jury's back.* Then, ten minutes later, *Guilty on all counts.*

I showed the message to Amanda, who squeezed my arm. "So it's finally over," she said. "What happens to her now, I wonder?"

"Prison," I replied, taking her hand, "probably for the rest of her life. No matter how you look at it, Sally Howard is a cold-blooded murderer."

"It's sad, though, don't you think, how the Ashcroft woman took everything away from her? One minute she's living the beautiful life, the next…" She looked up at me and said, "Harry, I can't imagine what that must have been like for her."

Neither could I.

The trials of Victoria Ashcroft and Dr. Sally Howard had consumed the better part of six months, drawing national attention.

Victoria had been discovered two days after the confrontation at the chemical plant, unconscious and suffering from severe hypothermia on a muddy riverbank nearly ten miles downstream. After her fall into the sluice, she'd been swept out into the river where she managed to grab onto a fallen tree. Eventually, the tree became lodged against a small island, where she was found, delirious and barely alive by a fisherman.

After her rescue from the river, Victoria recovered quickly from her ordeal, though it seemed to have broken her defiant spirit. She cooperated fully with federal prosecutors, providing detailed testimony about her illegal dumping operations, the murders she'd committed, and the extensive network of corruption she'd built throughout Hamilton County. Hers was a quick trial. She pled guilty to seventeen federal charges, including the murders of Dr. Jennifer Parker and her own father, conspiracy to commit environmental terrorism, racketeering, bribery, and the systematic poisoning of the Tennessee River.

Victoria was sentenced to life without parole on the murder charges, plus an additional forty years on the environmental and corruption charges.

Dr. Hensley cut a deal and cooperated with the US attorney in exchange for a reduced sentence. She received five years in federal prison.

Sally Howard's case had been more complex. It raised difficult questions about vigilante justice and the morality of revenge. She pled guilty to five counts of first-degree murder, but her defense team argued for leniency based on her cooperation with federal authorities and the environmental benefits of her financial warfare against Victoria's operation.

We learned two days later, on Friday morning, that she was sentenced to twenty-five years to life, with the possibility of parole after fifteen years. The judge acknowledged her cooperation and the environmental benefits of her actions, but said that vigilante justice cannot be tolerated regardless of the motivation.

"How did she take it?" I asked Kate that same afternoon.

"Calmly," Kate replied. "She said she accomplished what she set out to do, and she seemed at peace with the consequences."

As AMANDA, Jade, and I continued our visit to the aquarium, Jade, who was holding my hand, looked up at me and said, "Daddy, what happened to the lady who hurt Neptune?"

I looked at Amanda. She raised her eyebrows and shrugged, as if to say, 'That ball's in your court, Harry.'

"She's in prison," I said simply. "She can't hurt animals or people anymore."

"Good," Jade said with the simple moral clarity that only children possess.

If only it were that simple, I thought.

After walking Amanda to her car that afternoon, I drove to the police department. Kate had asked me to stop by for a final debriefing on the case. She was waiting in her office with Samson, surrounded by boxes of evidence that would soon be transferred to federal archives.

"How does it feel now that it's finally over?" she asked as I settled into the chair across from her desk.

"Complicated," I replied. "There's a lot to think about. It's going to take a while."

"Five deaths, massive environmental damage, and a crisis of faith," Kate said. "But it all worked out in the end, right?"

Samson rose lazily from his bed under the window, strolled over to where I was sitting and nudged my arm with his nose. I scratched behind his ears.

"Yes, I suppose it did," I said. "They're both in prison, so that's good, but I can't help but think about Sally, and the way her life was torn apart, her world turned upside down, the day Victoria killed her partner. Now look where she is, and will be for at least twenty years. And I have to wonder why. She was right, you know. About our system of justice. If she hadn't done what she did, Victoria would still be doing what she was doing."

"She certainly loved Jennifer, and she wanted to see justice done," Kate replied. "But murder? Uh uh! That's never the answer. You've said it yourself, many times."

"Oh, I know that," I said. "That's not what I'm saying. What I'm saying is, there has to be a better way, a way for people like her to get more easily to people like you."

It was at that moment that the door opened and Chief Johnston walked in, looking his usual 'all business' self.

"Harry," he said, "I want to thank you again for your work on this case. Your help was invaluable, as always," said, almost grudgingly, and I couldn't help but smile at him.

"Just doing my job, Chief," I replied.

"No, you weren't," Johnston said firmly. "You went above and beyond, again, just as you did when I lost Emily. Why the hell you ever left the force is beyond me."

"No, it isn't, Chief," I replied. "You know why I left. It was because of the BS, mostly from the same people in local government that put pressure on you during this investigation. But I'm always ready to help when I can. It's my civic duty."

"Yes," he said, "and I apologize for that. Some of us were more concerned about protecting the city's reputation than seeking justice for the victims. That's got to change, but it won't happen in my lifetime, unfortunately. Thanks again, Harry." And he turned abruptly and walked out the door, closing it behind him. And, after giving Samson a last pat on the head, I rose to my feet, saying, "It's time I went, Kate. Anything else you want to say?"

"Oh, plenty," she replied with a smile, "but it will keep. Come on, I'll walk you to your car."

And she did. Samson, too.

"So, what's next for you, Harry?" she asked as I put my hand on the door handle.

"Me? I need to get a grip on what's going on in my world," I replied. "I've leaned heavily on Jacque these last several months. It's time I pulled my weight."

"But you'll still help out if I need you, right?"

I grinned at her. "Of course," I said. "But try to keep the next case simple—a straightforward murder with clear motives and obvious suspects."

Kate laughed. "Then I wouldn't need you, would I?"

"Good point," I replied.

———

IF YOU ENJOYED this please take a moment to recommend this book. You can leave a review, share your thoughts on social media, or simply tell your friends and family. Keep reading for more murder mystery.

Harry Starke, Book 1 in the best-selling series, is a story of crime and corruption at the highest political levels, a mystery that plunges readers into a world where justice comes at a price, and the truth is the most dangerous weapon of all.

———

Thank you for reading Hunter's Moon. We hope you enjoyed this story. If this is your first book from Blair Howard may we suggest Harry Starke: Book One of the Harry Starke Private Investigator Novel Series, or Jasmine: Book One of the Lt. Kate Gazzara Murder Files.

If you would like a signed paperback head over to www.blairhowardbooks.com

WAYS TO GET NOTIFIED OF NEW RELEASES:
Follow on Amazon, BookBub, and join the authors email list.
SIGN UP For Announcements & great deals from the author on his website!

All Paperbacks are signed and priced at $9.99!
Get Exclusive Deals (As Part Of "The Family")
Visit www.BlairHowardBooks.com

The next pages provide a full overview of Blair Howard's fictional work.

Short Stories and Novellas

Buried Secrets(Harry Starke)

The Painted Lady(Kate Gazzara)

Stand Alone

Hunter's Moon(Kate & Harry)

Series

The Harry Starke Genesis Series

9 Books in Series as of 2025

The Harry Starke Series

26 Books in Series as of October 2025

The Lt. Kate Gazzara Murder Files

22 Books in Series as of October 2025

Randall And Carver Mysteries

4 Books in Series as of October 2025

The Peacemaker Series

3 Books in Series as of October 2025

The O'Sullivan Chronicles: Civil War Series

5 Books in Series as of October 2025

Science Fiction From Blair C. Howard

The Sovereign Star Series

7 Books in Series as of October 2025

also available in German

The Predecessors Series

The Last Station-Book One

The Infinity War-Book Two

ABOUT THE AUTHOR

 Blair Howard is the international best-selling author of more than seventy novels that span the worlds of gritty detective fiction, espionage thrillers, sweeping historicals, and hard-science military space opera. A Royal Air Force veteran and former journalist, he draws upon a rich background of service and storytelling to breathe life into unforgettable characters such as ex-cop turned private eye Harry Starke, and the fiercely determined homicide detective Lt. Kate Gazzara, who breaks her own trail as the head of a serious-crimes unit.

Under his sci-fi pen name Blair C. Howard, he expands his reach into the cosmos with the Sovereign Stars saga—an epic journey born from his lifelong love of the heavens, and the Predecessors hard science fiction trilogy. Whether unraveling a brutal crime scene or commanding starships in interstellar conflict, his stories are propelled by relentless pacing, vivid realism, and a watchful eye for justice.

Visit www.blairhowardbooks.com.
Email: BlairHoward@BlairHowardBooks.com

You can also find Blair Howard on Social Media

Made in United States
Orlando, FL
21 October 2025

71143727R10128